A VOYAGE FRAUGHT WITH PERIL:
THE CAPTAIN, LINDA AND THE TIGER SHARK

A VOYAGE FRAUGHT WITH PERIL:
THE CAPTAIN, LINDA AND THE TIGER SHARK

Their Love Was His Armor

CARLOS M. LAGO

MILL CITY PRESS

Mill City Press, Inc.
2301 Lucien Way #415
Maitland, FL 32751
407.339.4217
www.millcitypress.net

© 2019 by Carlos M. Lago

All rights reserved. No part of this publication may be reproduced, stored in a retrieval system, or transmitted, in any form or by any means, electronic, mechanical, photocopying, recording, or otherwise, without the prior written permission of the author.

Printed in the United States of America

ISBN-13: 978-1-54565-845-1

TABLE OF CONTENTS

Part I—The Captain

Chapter 1: The Captain Thinks about
            his Past and Present................1

Chapter 2: The Captain's Friends 9

Chapter 3: The Beginning of a Perilous Voyage...19

Chapter 4: Linda 27

Chapter 5: Storm Clouds Cast a Shadow
            on Their Love 33

Chapter 6: Freakish Happenings on Board.......37

Part II—The Tiger Shark

Chapter 7: Mario's Personal Experience
            with Sharks 41

Chapter 8: A History of Predation 51

Chapter 9: The Rogue Shark Searches
            for the Esperanza.................59

Chapter 10: His Daily Life on Board /
          Makes his Decision 65

Chapter 11: Duel on the Gulf Stream 83

Chapter 12: The Getaway 87

Part III–Breakthrough

Chapter 13: A New Life 91

Chapter 14: Life in His New Home 95

Chapter 15: Finally, There is Hope 99

Chapter 16: Return 103

Chapter 17: Aftermath 109

Appendix: The Tiger Sharks 113

Chapter 1
THE CAPTAIN THINKS ABOUT HIS PAST AND PRESENT

Mario Fernandez is his name. He was born in Cuba. His friends in Cuba called him by his nickname of "Captain." The reason is that he was in charge of the family's boat, and from the start, he had been its only captain. He felt great pride in that, for he loved boats. He is single, stands less than six feet tall, has brown hair and green eyes, and at that time was in his late twenties. Mario has a five-year Cuban high school education and comes across as being strong, smart, goal-oriented, and the kind of person who makes friends easily.

Christopher Columbus discovered Cuba in 1492. Title to an extensive land grant was awarded by Charles V, the Holy Roman Emperor and King of Spain, to Don Tomas Fernandez for bravery in fighting the French army during the 1494 to 1559 "Italian Wars" with France.

The Fernandez family is not well off. It's middle class. The family hailed from Northern Spain. Their land holdings had once been extensive, but various

Cuban governments at different times had taken advantage of their political clout to slice off big sections of their original land grant. They had done so without any form of compensation or actual purchase, leaving the family with ownership of only a small remnant of the original acreage.

The family worked the land, growing crops mostly for their own consumption and seeking to be as self-sufficient as possible. Food was hard to secure in communist Cuba, so their approach made sense. The Cuban Revolutionary government had not taken their land because it was a very small tract. Although the family members did not believe in Castro-Communism, they were not perceived as being violent opponents of the Castro regime who would try to foment counter-revolution. The Fernandez family members were good friends and neighbors. They did not discuss politics with their neighbors, nor meddle in anyone else's business, and were always available to lend a hand in harvesting their neighbors' crops.

One good thing about the Fernandez land was that it extended into the beach area and accessed the reef. His father had bought, secondhand, a small boat years ago. Family members would often don their skin-diving gear (principally, masks and flippers) and swim out to spearfish around the reef. Sometimes they were lucky and managed to catch a large red snapper or an occasional lobster or two. The seafood provided needed animal protein and served to supplement the produce they harvested from their land. Mario especially loved the family's boat and learned all he could about its navigation and also developed some expertise in boat engine repair.

The Captain Thinks about his Past and Present

Mario was a lover of the heavens since childhood. He owned a small telescope inherited from his grandfather and used it very often. The moon was a favorite viewing subject of his. It never failed to impress Mario, especially when observing it through his telescope. It's our nearest neighbor in space: big, bright, and beautiful, and just a quarter of a million miles away. Fortunately, the clear Cuban skies offered the very best viewing of the moon and the planets. Mario could name at least a dozen of the moon's surface features just by using his unaided eyes.

Mario is endowed with the muscle mass, skill, and endurance typical of farmers and fishermen accustomed to toiling long hours on the field and at sea in very difficult conditions. All persons who make their living from the ocean risk their lives every single day. Mario is blessed with the intelligence and diligence to tackle many difficult situations. When he is happy or amused, he displays a most disarming smile that is genuine, warm, and inviting. He is a great storyteller, ready and able to entertain his audience with tales of his adventures at sea.

The term "Cuban exiles" refers to the many Cubans who departed their homeland because of communism. It consisted of mostly middle class and upper class Cubans who left to preserve their individual liberty and rights. Some left because they feared widespread reprisals and devastating property seizures by the Marxist government of Fidel Castro. Others gladly left the island for the privilege of living as free people in a free country; the Cuban exiles in this group were mainly seeking political asylum. Many of Castro's supporters who had remained in Cuba ultimately ended up fleeing the island when they perceived Fidel's communist intentions. Between 1959 and 1970, half a million Cubans left the country.

In Cuba, Mario felt as if his world was shrinking. Everyone had to profess fidelity to the Castro regime, learn about communism, and serve Cuba's revolutionary government and state. He concluded that personal freedom had been buried forever. Mario had plans to leave the island and test his wings in America as soon as possible.

In the early days of the Castro regime, Cubans could travel unimpeded everywhere. The government encouraged it because, if the travelers did not return home, the government would confiscate all they owned. Mario's mother, Esperanza, who was very religious, went to church daily and prayed that her son Mario would stay home with them. If he, nonetheless, had decided to leave Cuba, Esperanza planned to give him a special gift.

The Fernandez family members did not want to say their goodbyes to Mario at the airport. It was not a private enough space, and there would be some tears shed. So, it was done in their home. Esperanza cooked a wonderful dinner in Mario's honor, and they spent most of the night talking, sharing photos and many embraces. The following morning, Esperanza took her son aside, handed him the most cherished piece of jewelry she owned, her wedding ring, and asked that it be used as the engagement ring he would give his future wife. Mario accepted lovingly, gratefully.

Mario's father thought differently than his mother about Mario's departure. He loved his son but also understood his wishes and his needs, and was not opposed to his departure if that would make him a happy man. They already had two sons and a daughter, so their loss of one family member, although very sad, would not be unbearable.

His parents gave Mario dollars they had saved from the time when a Cuban peso was worth as much as a US dollar. Mario arrived in Miami as a passenger in one of the flights leaving the island. The exiles left behind all they owned, but on the positive side, they also left behind jails full of opponents of the regime — a Marxist government that controlled everything: what to eat, what to think, what to read, where to live, who his friends should be, where to pray, or not, and many more restrictions.

He promised his parents and other family members that he would write them often and send them needed food and medicines. He was certain that his family would remain in Cuba no matter what, for the Fernandez family had lived in Cuba for centuries and had no interest in leaving. Some of his ancestors had left their mark in the pages of Cuban history. Mario knew that his parents and siblings would not travel to Florida to see him.

Since first landing in the United States, he had found affection and genuine generosity. This country had accepted Mario as a refugee from communist Cuba. He became, with time, a naturalized American citizen. In Cuba, his father had taught him all about their boat, and it was fortunate that he had done so, because his son's knowledge of boats would allow him to make a living in the US. It would not be an overstatement to say that boats were such an important part of Mario's identity as a person that it would be very hard for him to work away from boats.

It was obvious to him that he should try to get a job as a marine mechanic, a type of handy man who could fix boats and repair engines. He had a natural, God-given mechanical talent that came handy in working on his friends' boats. He learned a lot on the job and managed to earn a living. He remembered his father's words that education had to be his first goal, for that was the only thing no government could ever take away from him. When an employer, a marina, impressed by the quality of his work, offered to pay for his night school training as a marine mechanic, he happily and gratefully accepted. He wanted his new friends and acquaintances to call him by the nickname of "Captain," and that is how he will be addressed in this writing.

The Captain saved his money to purchase a boat with a cabin and twin outboard motors. He also planned to purchase a dinghy that he could use if the boat was ever in peril of sinking. He could not purchase them now without securing a bank loan, which he did. He had spent a lot of time and effort locating such a boat and also in researching the right motors for his dinghy. The motors had to have plenty of power and ease in starting up. He had first considered gas-powered outboards but thought they were not very reliable. In the end, he chose electric rather than gas.

The boat he purchased was large enough to accommodate four paying customers, who would sleep on extra-special, comfortable bunk beds. The boat functioned mainly as a charter fishing craft. His usual customers departed from Tampa and flew or drove to Miami to board his boat, which he named "Esperanza" for his mother. The word means "hope" in Spanish. His customers were well off and were welcome on his ten-day fishing trips. The Captain was a very good cook and provided delicious meals for his customers. Another plus was that the paying guests would be taken back home while still catching fish. Word-of-mouth helped, and there were many repeat customers.

Recently, he had found the perfect dinghy for his boat. It not only fulfilled his needs, but he never would have to worry about its keel getting stuck in the sandy bottom, for the motor could be tilted up to an elevated position, either electronically or manually. He named the dinghy "Pescadito," which means "little fish" in Spanish.

Chapter 2
THE CAPTAIN'S FRIENDS

A marina is a dock or basin providing secure mooring for pleasure and fishing boats, and also offering the latest in boats and marine engines, and functions also as a reliable supplier of parts. Besides these benefits, boat owners could always rely on the expertise of the mechanics there to service their needs. The "Marina" was the official name of the company where he works. One could tell by the chosen name that its owner definitely had a sense of humor. It was more than a place customers visited to buy boat parts or to fix their boats and engines. The Marina also owned a cafeteria where clients and employees would gather to get something to eat or drink.

The employees at the cafeteria were the cooks, bar tenders, and waitresses who prepared the food and waited on tables. The Marina's owner did his best to hire the most qualified employees. He thought that if the cafeteria became a success, customers would hang around longer and perhaps do additional business with them. The Marina's cafeteria was seated on the beach itself, and those customers sitting along the terrace enjoyed the touch of the cool ocean breezes. They also enjoyed the beauty of the swaying palm trees, the rolling waves, and the ballet gyrations of the sea birds as they glided above the waves on the wings of the wind.

It is mid-day, and the Captain is having his lunch at one of the tables facing the beach. The tide is low, and the moon is barely visible. The Captain has a best friend, Andrew Stevens, who he calls Andy. They are having lunch together and talking about their future plans and objectives.

The Captain met him one day by chance when Andy was talking to a boat owner, and the Captain overheard a few sentences that intrigued him. The topic of conversation had been the coming improvements in boat technology, and that topic was extremely interesting to the Captain. He politely introduced himself and became engrossed in technical conversation with Andy. It was as if they had been life-long friends sharing a hobby. The Captain found out that Andy was born in the US. His parents, unable to put up with Chicago's weather, had moved to Florida. Andy was also an expert marine mechanic. The Captain thought they could eventually be partners, working together in fixing up boats and repairing boat engines. Andy also liked the idea, and eventually, the two of them became partners.

Andy was a happy man, an honest, hard-working, steadfast friend. He had a lighter side than the Captain and told him jokes that would make the Captain smile. Andy was single but dating. He would join the Captain occasionally when both of them had some free time to spare. Then, they would canvass the area looking for potential clients in need of expert boat mechanics. They traveled along the Gulf of Mexico and up the East

The Captain's Friends

coast all the way to North Carolina's better marinas and developed important contacts in those places. They were very much in demand.

There was a young lady the Captain would have loved to meet. One day at lunch, he told Andy that he thought he had seen an angel because her hair was golden, like the sun, like hay, and her eyes were like baby-blue aquamarines. That was how Andy found out that the Captain was madly in love. The Captain knew at what time of day she came down to the Cafeteria for lunch, and he'd turn his head and search until he spotted her. Andy now knew which lady the Captain was pining for. She was Linda Smith, a new Marina employee with an important job.

One day when Linda sat at her table, she noticed a man looking at her and found herself looking back at him and smiling. That's something she would not have done at all under normal circumstances, but in this instance, she allowed it to happen because she was strangely drawn to this man. She thought his smile was captivating and that he was a ruggedly handsome and attractive man. Just as she suspected, the stranger's eyes never left her face because, every few minutes, he would sneak a side look at her. However, she did not feel uneasy or threatened by his attention.

Linda hailed from the state of Alabama. To the Captain's eyes, she was lovely. Andy heard that she was hired to work on improving the Marina's cash flow and also to review the financial health of the organization as recorded in their financial ledgers. It was an important job. She was smart and personable and also beautiful. Andy asked around and found out that Linda was single and immediately told the Captain.

A VOYAGE FRAUGHT WITH PERIL: THE **CAPTAIN, LINDA** AND THE **TIGER SHARK**

One day, Linda was sitting at a nearby table in the Cafeteria and overheard them speaking Spanish. Andy was not a native speaker of Spanish, but he had learned good Spanish in school. Linda came over and introduced herself, and the Captain and Andy told her their names. After sharing small talk, to his surprise and delight, Linda asked the Captain if he would teach her Spanish. She added she would pay for his time. The Captain was delighted and quickly replied, "Yes."

Linda came from a well-to-do family with southern traditions and refinement. She dressed well; was articulate, refined, and soft spoken; and had good manners. She did not come across as being snobbish or better than everyone else. Linda believed that the qualities of a person's feelings, his actions, his character, and beliefs were what really mattered in a man, not his ancestry and social status, nor his financial resources. She recognized in the Captain the very best qualities and a great potential for success. Not to be underestimated, there was also a strong spark of attraction between them that often made her blush. The Captain and Linda met once a week in the Marina's cafeteria, at a table they had reserved. The regular customers started to notice how close the two of them had become over time. The day of the class, both Linda and the Captain dressed well and looked their very best. Sometimes, as he tried to explain certain words, by happenstance their hands touched, and very powerful feelings were aroused, which they managed to conceal and restrain.

At first, they both pulled back their hands, but later on, they did not avoid contact. One May afternoon, when the grounds were awash with colorful flowers and the crowds had left the cafeteria, the Captain asked

Linda to translate a new phrase from Spanish to English. He wrote the following words: "Estas siempre en mi corazon." The words, translated from Spanish, mean, "You are always in my heart." Linda smiled and wrote down, "Y tu estas en el mio," which means, "And you are in mine." The Captain was overjoyed. He reached for Linda, and she did not object. Smiling, he looked into her eyes, held her in his arms, and they kissed softly and for a long time.

Every so often, the Captain would invite her to join him in his boat to visit some interesting places not too far away. They would swim and talk, and laugh together, learning more about each other. Their intimacy grew. They felt a deep affection and concern for each other. They knew they were deeply in love. He sent her flowers every week with attached notes affirming his love for her. They talked long hours on the phone, often beyond midnight.

It was not the first time that Linda and the Captain had experienced the intensity of falling in love with someone. When they fell in love for the first time, as teenagers, they learned what it feels like to love someone intensely and unconditionally. They had been lucky, for when their romance ended, they still remained as good friends with their partners. Many circumstances beyond their control had affected their teenage relationships and determined their next steps in life. In fact, they had drifted apart from each other's sweethearts without having suffered the emotional trauma of being dumped by their beloved for someone else's love.

The Captain and Linda had previously learned to put their egos aside and to grow together with their partner. This loving feeling between the Captain and Linda was deep and growing deeper with every passing day. It was not an infatuation; it was love between two mature individuals. That love did not mean expecting to spend every waking minute together or being co-dependent. In truth, they had a healthy relationship, one between equals. As was to be expected of two persons in love, they had deeply connected with each other and were open to learn of each other's problems. Problems that unexpectedly arose were solved by them working as a team. Linda told her parents that she had a special bond with the Captain and that they were very much in love.

She wanted to introduce him to classical music but found out that there was really no need of that, because the Captain already knew about the symphonic and piano classical masterpieces. Ruben Fernandez, the Captain's father, owned an extensive collection of classical music in thirty-three rpm long-playing vinyl records that he played constantly on his record player. The Captain's favorite classical composers were Beethoven, Ravel, and Tchaikovsky. In semi-classical, he favored the music of Cuban composer Ernesto Lecuona.

The Captain did not know much about opera, never really considered it. Together with Andy, he regularly made fun of the overweight sopranos appearing on television shows. Linda, who was very much an opera expert, did her best to convince him to ignore the hefty sopranos' looks and enjoy their marvelous voices instead. When she sweetly asked him to become an opera fan, he said, "Yes," but only if it could be kept a secret from Andy and his Marina friends.

The Captain and Linda attended several opera performances, and Linda boasted to the Smiths, her parents, that the Captain was becoming an opera "buff"

The Captain's Friends

through her guidance. He particularly loved the operas of Puccini. Linda also told her parents that the Captain had a great knowledge of classical music. They were fully surprised.

The Captain wished to invite Linda to dinner at his home. He had never done that for other young women he had dated. This desire showed the Captain that his relationship with Linda was not casual dating but was developing into a more serious commitment on his part. He thought he knew her more deeply now and wanted to be with her as often as they could arrange it. It had happened slowly, imperceptibly, and its realization took him by surprise.

Something similar was taking place with Linda. She realized that she wanted to be with the Captain. When she talked with her mother about some of her weekly activities, they invariably included her dates with the Captain. She told her mother that she had known him for only three weeks but was having trouble remembering what her life had been like prior to their meeting.

A friend once told her that relationships were like accidents: you don't find them; they find you. When Linda told her mother that he had invited her to dinner at his home, her mother remarked that she thought their relationship had grown from simply dating to a more serious courting, and that the Captain was close to making a decision about proposing to her. Linda was very hopeful that it would happen as foretold.

The day of the dinner date, the Captain opened the front door to his home and invited Linda inside. He prepared the meal in the kitchen, and after dessert and a glass of wine, they entered the Captain's garden. It was a beautiful night, and the moon was full and cast a romantic spell over the gathering. Because the Captain's home was not far away from the ocean, a soft, cool breeze from the sea meandered around them. The scent of the surf lingered in the air.

The garden he'd planted surrounded the central patio of his house on all sides. A marble fountain graced its very center. He was justifiably proud of it. Tonight, he had showcased the flowering plants with patio lights.

Linda could tell that he loved roses. He had planted the best ones he could afford to buy, for roses were his parents' favorite flowers. The rose flowers brought him happy memories of his past family life in Cuba. The Captain also loved the heady fragrance of gardenia and jasmine and planted them near the roses, and each night their combined fragrance wafted up and all around, enveloping the pair. It was a shame that it was dark already, because the hummingbirds would not be flitting about; they'd be sleeping in their tiny nests. He wished he could have shown them off to Linda in the midst of their spectacular, colorful ballets staged around his blooming plants.

In his Cuban garden, dazzling, multicolored hummingbirds would be seen daily, sipping nectar while suspended in the air with their beaks inside the many flowers. He remembered that their wings moved so incredibly fast that they made a humming sound, becoming practically invisible to the naked eye. His mother once had remarked that the ruby-throated hummingbirds looked like a group of thirsty little girls in their pretty red dresses, sipping strawberry ice cream soda.

Linda looked up and saw that the heavens seemed to have flowered on her first visit there, not with blossoms, but with trillions of brightly shining stars. She thought the setting could not have been more romantic.

On his flowering trees, the Captain had fastened orchids with gorgeous flowers, especially the fragrant ones. Fragrant cattleyas were his favorite orchids and also the colorful multicolored ascocendas and the yellow oncidiums. Phalaenopsis orchids, with their long, arching spikes of many flowers in all colors, were the most popular orchids in Florida. One would find them growing in pots everywhere. The Captain liked phalaenopsis hybrids because they were showy in a graceful, self-assured way, but he loved fragrance in flowers and would have loved them more if the flowers had had a pleasing scent. Linda also loved them and kept a few of them in her home.

Linda and the Captain enjoyed sitting in chairs around a white metal outdoor table, holding hands. The table was deliberately placed under the shade of a beautiful tropical Flamboyant tree (*Delonix regia*). The Captain had planted it from seed. The seed had come from the Captain's family garden in Cuba. Linda loved that tree. When it flowered, it was a vision of loveliness, with its multitude of splendid orchid-like flowers colored a fiery red.

His small house was a fixer-upper by the shore. He'd bought it with some cash he had saved, but mostly through a loan from the local bank. He faithfully paid his mortgage down every month. The Captain was gradually improving his home to suit his needs. He saved money by fishing and eating the fish he caught. The fish came from beyond the reef that stretched out in a straight line like a piece of rope laid down parallel to the shore.

A VOYAGE FRAUGHT WITH PERIL: THE **CAPTAIN, LINDA** AND THE **TIGER SHARK**

At the rear of his property, concealed by an out-of-the-way grove of bamboo, he had planted lettuce, tomatoes, pumpkin, corn, and sweet potatoes. He had built a hen house so he could eat chicken. He harvested eggs and sold them to a nearby grocery store. Because his income had gone up, he now had funds to invest, but as he knew nothing about investments, he decided instead to spend some of his cash in making additional payments on his loans and also buying needed furniture for his home.

Occasionally, the Captain would untie his dinghy from the pier and climb aboard. He did his best thinking while riding the waves. Today the tide was low, and the dinghy's keel almost scraped the sandy bottom. He saw stingrays and crabs scrambling in all directions. An immense sun blazed above, and the glare blinded him so much that he shielded his eyes with the palm of one hand. He could barely make out the moon's cratered face. Most of the fish were hiding under the reef. He thought that if he were fishing he'd catch nothing much. The reflection of sunlight from the water became unbearably strong. He shut his eyes and looked away. His mind digressed. He saw lobsters milling around chunks of coral and thought that a lobster trap could do well there. Linda was now fully on his mind, and he wondered if he should phone to invite her to dine in a Miami restaurant that was famous for their fresh seafood. He knew that Linda loved stone crabs and was sure she would enjoy eating them, for they were a very special gourmet treat of the season.

Chapter 3
THE BEGINNING OF A PERILOUS VOYAGE

The Captain had dropped his paying customers, mostly sports fishermen, in Tampa, home for many of them. He knew all of them very well, because they were good, faithful customers of his. Sometimes they'd invite the Captain to their homes and introduce him to their wife and kids, and the children would invariably ask him to tell them some of the interesting sights the Captain had seen. They knew their father periodically would fly down to Miami to join a fishing excursion planned by the Captain on his boat, Esperanza.

The port was bustling with activity as ships arrived and departed in a steady flow. There were cruise ships at anchor, waiting for the best tide and wind conditions before departing the safety of the port. The weather had become hot and sultry; even the sea breeze did not cool the port city. Hordes of mosquitoes, gnats, and biting flies had smelled his sweat and found it irresistible. They were whining in his ear and trying to feed.

A VOYAGE FRAUGHT WITH PERIL: THE **CAPTAIN**, **LINDA** AND THE **TIGER SHARK**

He was now ready to navigate the Esperanza toward home. The voyage along the west coast of Florida from Tampa was uneventful. The sea was calm, the weather ideal, and no strong winds materialized to slow down his voyage. Soon enough, his boat rounded the tip of Florida, and the Captain was a happy man because he would soon be with Linda, his sweetheart.

As soon as he'd done that, the sky turned dark, the sea turned choppy, and the waves loomed large and strong. There was a mist that soon became a fog. The fog floated in the air and thickened, blocking some of the sunlight from reaching the boat. He thought the ensuing dark shadows seemed out of place, otherworldly, and worrisome.

At this moment, the Captain thought the furious ocean was an irascible and indifferent deity. Torrents of rain lashed down noisily on the deck. The wind shrieked like hundreds of souls in torment. There were blinding bolts of lightning that materialized directly overhead. The boat slid down the slope of a wave and up the crest of another but with difficulty. The motors strained against the force of the waves. He realized the Esperanza had been ambushed by a tropical squall the likes of which he had never before experienced.

The waves kept building up in size and power, with white foam crowning the peaks. The wind skimmed white foam off the crest of the waves and spread it all over the deck, reminding the Captain of a shifting landscape covered by the whiteness of snow. Massive swells played with the boat, and the rain came down fast and hard. It felt strange to be suddenly terrified of this ocean, gone berserk! The Captain had never experienced anything like the ferocity and overwhelming violence of this storm. Waves that exist in the center of a storm are true avalanches of water, monstrous waves piled up on top of huge waves, all of them rushing forward in a mission of total destruction. High above, the lightning flashed, and the wind gushed in pulses, pushing against the boat's gunwales with such force that at times it nearly succeeded in capsizing the Esperanza.

As the waves rushed the boat from all sides, the Captain steered to take them head on. The boat became hostage to the waves, the wind, and the currents, tossed to one side or the other. Then, as it crested a huge wave, the outboard motors sputtered out. The Captain suspected the wave had lifted the propellers out of the water, allowing them to spin freely and causing a total shut down. As a result, the boat's movement slowed down and soon came to a sudden stop. Unfortunately for the Captain, the squall had made radio communication unfeasible during and after the storm, and no help would be forthcoming. At a distance, the storm walked off on blue bolts of lightning, and was gone.

Afterward, he imagined seeing his father standing by his side, sharing the voyage with him. His father's image somehow infused him with extra strength and spiritual support. He did not feel so alone anymore. The Captain could do nothing more to remedy his present situation. Night had fallen, and looking up at the sky, he saw the splendor of trillions of stars blazing above and thought of God. He also remembered that, nightly in Cuba, he had trained his telescope on the moon, the planets, and the nearest stars.

The moon was his usual target. He would spend evenings looking at its cratered face and following the moon's phases and eclipses. He could spot and name at least a dozen of its surface features with the unaided eye. Binoculars showed him scores more, and a telescope kept him busy on the moon, nonstop.

Tonight, a moon the color of cream hung over the ocean. The entire scene looked magical: the light of the moon was reflected on the slow waves and bathed the tops of the swells in softest light. In spite of the horror of his ordeal, having braved and experienced nature at its wildest, the Captain found himself harboring tender thoughts about the moon.

The moon, an old friend, so delicately feminine and yet powerful enough to create the ocean tides, moving huge masses of seawater all over the world and affecting the weather and the reproductive cycles of humans, plants, and animals. It was a display of its many powers. He felt a curious bond with the moon, but the moon, although lovely, looked lonely and remote to him on his first night of drifting. Under his feet, the boat moved silently, aimlessly, over a deep and pitch-dark ocean.

He recalled that scientists theorized that the moon had once been part of earth that had spun out into space eons ago. The Captain thought the moon had class, an undeniable majesty. It ruled over the night sky. He said, to no one in particular, "Why not call her Queen of the Night Sky?" In his reverie, he thought it was the earth's doing that the moon was retreating from our planet, some say about an inch and a half each year. The Captain could not help but fully sympathize with the moon. He thought of the moon as a bride, all dressed up in bridal white, only to be rejected at the altar by our planet. He looked for answers to a troubling question: "Why was earth pushing my beautiful moon away?"

"PENNY"

The Captain owned a small dog, a Havanese breed, cute and frisky. It was a gift from his mother, Esperanza. She owned a pair of Havanese dogs in Cuba, male and female, and had given her son, as a birthday present, a puppy from a new litter. The Captain had chosen the puppy himself. It was cute and beautiful, very sociable, and loved to be held.

When the Captain left Cuba for good, he'd taken it with him on his flight to Miami. He named the puppy "Penny." He told friends in jest that the dog's name was Penny because he had spent a pretty penny to purchase it (not true), and also because a penny is small, and so was his dog. He had brought Penny along on his voyage to Tampa and enjoyed its company. His paying customers also raved about the puppy, and the wives, if present, cuddled and babied Penny at all times and rewarded it with treats.

The Havanese dogs are very small dogs, some less than twelve inches tall, taken by Spanish traders to Cuba. They became popular as pets of the elite and as performing dogs. A few of the dogs remained in Cuba, and it is known that three families with their Havanese pet dogs left Cuba for the United States during the 1950s and the 1960s. Most present-day Havanese dogs are thought to be true descendants of these dogs. They are busy, curious dogs, happiest when they are the center of attention. These dogs love to play and clown, and each one is affectionate with its owner, with strangers, and with other dogs and pets.

Penny followed the Captain around wherever he went. At night, it slept at the end of the Captain's bed and made a nest for itself within the blankets. When on deck, it would chase the seabirds until they flew away, and the Captain thought that was a plus because Penny would not allow any of them to leave a "deposit" on his deck. The ladies thought it was cute to watch the puppy in action. Penny was true company for the Captain and entertainment for the guests.

The Captain noticed that the boat was now drifting faster and deduced that it was likely caught within the strong current of warmer seawater known as the Gulf Stream. The current was carrying his boat north and west, almost parallel to the US East coast. Night fell, and he walked around the deck looking up at the moon and the stars. He thought he saw a shooting star and believed it would be a good luck omen.

The Captain was fatigued by the recent happenings. The boat was without power and drifting on the current, and there was nothing else he could do to help. He observed that there was a glow in the water surrounding the Esperanza. He would have stayed longer on deck but was exhausted and decided to turn in for the night. He quickly fell asleep and dreamt he was awake, enjoying the magical spectacle of phosphorescence in the waters below and around the boat due to billions of plankton life forms, bacteria, jellyfish, and trillions of protozoans, and all were suddenly ablaze! As fish swam around and below, they left behind a fiery trail, and outlines of the fish glowered like fireflies against the impenetrable darkness.

In his dream, he saw a black marlin armored in blue-green light spring clear out of the water, chased

The Beginning of a Perilous Voyage

by a massive predator. The Captain hoped the black marlin would outrace the shark, for he guessed the predator had been an attacking shark. It must have eluded the shark somehow, for peace now reigned supreme all around his boat. The show of lights went on: porpoises jumped out of the water in unison, and foam that looked like lava slid off their backs. The pod of porpoises sensed the approach of something threatening and quickly disappeared. The Captain's dream came to a sudden stop when he felt two sharp blows to the side of the boat that made his alarm clock fall off the night table. The clock loudly hit the floor and caused Penny to bark nonstop. The Captain stood up and quickly walked up to the deck. Looking out over the waves, he saw nothing to worry about.

After that, he felt no more impacts, and the Captain speculated that perhaps a floating log was to blame. He also considered if the impacts were the work of something altogether different, and dreadful. Perhaps the storm had dredged up from the depths a noxious being, someone powerful and malevolent, capable of venting its fury on the boat's hull and on its passenger. His inner voice sounded the alarm, but he was too weary and worn out to acknowledge it. The Captain returned to his quarters, lay down on the bed, rested his head on his pillow, closed his eyes, and fell fast asleep.

Chapter 4
LINDA

The piercing light of the midday sun was no match for the heavy velvet curtains framing the windows in the Captain's bedroom. They had been strategically placed so that only a reduced amount of light was allowed inside. The dark furniture and the blue Persian rug also helped to soak any of the surplus light. Linda thought the room looked cozy. There were bookcases along one wall totally full of books. The books had been bound with hardcovers of different colors. When stacked up vertically against each other, edgewise, the effect was as if small rainbows were living within the bookcases, emanating a feeling of calm and quiet contentment. Somehow, it seemed to Linda, the curtains within the room held the better pieces of the Captain's past, managing to exclude painful memories of his exodus from Cuba. She had plenty of time to go over in her mind how they had met. Linda had seen him often at the Marina's cafeteria. Their eyes had met, and they both had smiled. She had hoped then that they would meet in person one fine day, and they had.

A VOYAGE FRAUGHT WITH PERIL: THE **CAPTAIN, LINDA** AND THE **TIGER SHARK**

The Captain was attracted to blondes, and the reason may have been that there were fewer blonde women in Cuba, but also because, to him, they looked very alluring. She was three years younger than the Captain, came from a large old family rooted in Alabama, and her name was Linda Smith. She had not enrolled in an exclusive finishing school her mother suggested. Instead, she had attended the best of secretarial schools because she wanted to be independent of the whims of her parents. At the school, she learned to type and take dictation and also learned accounting and bookkeeping. It was almost certain that she would be able to support herself, be fully independent, and an asset to any business or corporation. The Marina quickly offered her a job.

But there were afternoons when her job felt too arid to her liking, with too many numbers, and columns, and formulas all day long. She realized she needed to participate in more feminine pursuits after work. Her mother had paid for her voice lessons years ago in Birmingham, on the condition that she never would perform in public. She had also received lessons in dancing and poetic literature while in Birmingham. Linda wrote poetry and was told she was good at it. She asserted that writing poems was good for her soul and began to get creative once more.

The Captain and Linda were inseparable. It seemed they had found what they needed in each other. It was plain to everyone around that they were very much in love. They acted as if they were already married, to the extent that they often seemed to finish each other's sentences. Linda smiled a lot, and the Captain found her smile to be utterly captivating.

They went to the movies together, and on other weekend nights they dined out and went dancing at some of the hotels. Often, they double dated with Andy and his girlfriend. They'd also go sightseeing on some weekend trips. The Captain had met Linda's parents, and they knew his intentions were good; and beyond that, her parents admired the way he had made something of himself. He was courteous and charming with her parents, and they were favorably impressed. They knew about his past life in Cuba and his exodus to the US, and they did not disapprove of their joint plans for the future. Linda's parents had given the loving couple their blessing, but now they saw that their daughter was not wearing an engagement ring and looked unhappy, and it worried them.

The Captain's trust in Linda was complete. He gave her copies of his keys to the mailbox and his front door. When he was away on his boat, Linda helped him tie loose ends. Passing by the post office, she'd gather all his mail and then climb the stairs to his bedroom. She'd spread the mail on his night table, next to her framed photograph, and separated the letters into piles, starting from the seemingly most urgent and important ones to the least important, while reserving a tall pile for the trash mail.

She knew the Captain's return was overdue. Linda tried to allay her fears by telling herself that delays were often unavoidable when seamen were faced with the vagaries of wind, weather, and currents. To be sure of God's protection, Linda prayed that the Captain and his boat would be safe. One night she had a disturbing dream: she saw an empty garden lit by an enormous moon. It shone with a glacial light the color of mother-of-pearl, and the entire garden appeared totally bleached of color. She felt bitterly cold, and shivered uncontrollably under the sheets. Linda recognized it: the garden was the Captain's garden.

The colorful flowers she once loved were colorless now, sadly drained of their vibrant floral pigments, and the trees looked wilted and wan. The round metal table they sat by, and where they often held hands and kissed, had strangely disappeared. The white marble fountain was cracked and held no water. The familiar red cardinal in his nest on the peach tree by the fountain was all white now, and dead inside the nest. Somehow, birds in the trees couldn't sing a note, couldn't fly straight, and were the color of new ivory. All the trees displayed silver leaves on their branches and, if they bloomed at all, bloomed a pallid, waxen white. She saw that there was too much white in her dream, and she asked herself, "Could that be a forecast of tragic events to come?" The frightening thought occurred to her that hospitals and headstones in cemeteries were marble-white, and that was the new color of his garden. Linda feared that death had somehow found its way into the Captain's garden, their garden of love. She desperately looked for the Captain in her dream but did not find him there, or anywhere, and in anguish, she awoke with a jolt, sat down on the bed and wept, but could not stop.

The newspapers printed stories about tempests off the East coast that created sizeable destruction, wrecked homes, and flooded seaside towns, but she hoped the Captain had not met any of those. She yearned to be held by him! She told herself, "He will not be lost at sea. He'll come back for me!" Linda missed him, missed

Linda

his loving gaze, his embrace, his kisses. She missed the sound of his voice, his sense of humor.

They were so much in love! She once told her mother, proudly, that the Captain would dedicate all of his romantic love poems to her. He was popular; at the Marina, all the Captain's friends inquired about him. Unfortunately, she did not have news for them, and they, in turn, had no news to share with her.

Linda was opposed to his long voyages around Florida's coasts. She knew that the fishing industry was hazardous to fishermen, and the statistics were that in a seven-year time period, it had averaged seventy-eight deaths a year. Accidents at sea were common, but as long as the ships' crews were able to stay near their boats, they would survive. However, if the boat sank, it was often the sharks that took their lives. Linda and the Captain had talked about his upcoming voyage to Tampa and whether there would be additional fishing trips. She wanted the Captain to devote all of his time and effort to repairing boats and marine engines and remain safe, safe for her and for their future children.

Chapter 5
STORM CLOUDS CAST A SHADOW ON THEIR LOVE

Linda's parents were wealthy, part of the upper crust of high society families of Birmingham, Alabama. They owned a mansion in an exclusive residential area where just about the richest, smartest people of Birmingham made their home. The homes there were about three times as expensive as the state average, and the families earned far more than most people made in two or three years.

The Smith family owned real estate, stocks and bonds, and a profitable export/import business. Their business was headquartered in Mobile. They owned an apartment there where they could stay if needed. The Smiths wanted their daughter, Linda, to return home for various reasons, mainly because they loved and missed her, but they also wanted her to reintegrate herself into Birmingham's social life and their life. Besides that, they could use her help in managing their assets, especially on the financial side. She had expertise they thought they sorely needed.

Linda had an admirer in Birmingham, a young man who had dated her in high school and was in love with her. He had asked her parents about Linda. The Smiths hoped that once back in Birmingham and living in their home, she would fall in love with her admirer, marry, and decide to stay there permanently.

To her father, Linda's choice of a future husband was clearly unwise and disappointing. Linda's parents knew that the Captain was below Linda's social class. Her father thought there had been various actions Linda had taken in the recent past that were troubling and totally unexpected. For instance, Linda had enrolled in a secretarial school instead of an exclusive finishing school for young ladies her mother had attended. Questionable also were her decisions to live in Florida and work for a marina, and also her choice of future husband. They had decided not to intervene then, but years had passed and they saw that Linda and the Captain were not even engaged! They decided it was time for them to intervene.

They both came down to see her while the Captain was away and asked if she would consider returning to them and becoming a presence in their home, and their lives, once more. They also brought with them a Hallmark card from her admirer in Alabama. The card held his photograph and a short hand-written note where he said he'd love to come and see her again and included his phone number.

Linda considered all her options. She was not happy with the fact that she was not wearing the Captain's engagement ring, the special wedding ring that once had belonged to his dear mother, a ring that the Captain had promised her. When she had asked him about it, the

Captain had said that he could not find it and vouched he had looked everywhere. He told Linda that he'd continue looking. Linda did not know what to think or do. At times, she wanted to turn her back on her present life with the Captain and heed her parents' advice, but she also felt that she deeply loved the Captain and would not be happy away from him. She told her parents she would think about their offer, and they returned home full of hope.

Linda had already told the Captain her wish was for him to quit using his boat to cater to tourists by taking them out on fishing expeditions. She knew the dangers of being out on the ocean far away from land. As for the Captain, fishing had become second nature to him. He was proud of having been captain of his family's fishing boat in Cuba. The Captain saw that Linda could not understand that fishermen, sooner or later, fell in love with the sea. The ocean fed the fisherman, fed his body and soul. Fishing is a man's habit that's hard to break. His dear cousin was a fisherman, and he was still alive. The Captain would say to her, "Christ's disciples, saintly men who spread God's word, were all fishermen!"

Concerning his bank loans, the Captain had to make sure that the monthly home mortgage payment and the payment on the bank loans to purchase the Esperanza and the dinghy were paid to the bank on time when he was away in his boat. If he missed a couple of payments, the bank would surely re-possess his property. To prevent that from happening, he had asked Linda to do him the favor of making the payments when he was away by using dollars in a fund he had set up for that purpose.

The Captain was most concerned about her expressed doubts about the viability of their relationship, and how the doubts had grown in her mind to the extent that they now threatened the health and continuity of their love. He truly believed that their shared love, so genuine, so deep and real, would conquer all. He saw, however, that it needed additional care, emergency treatment right now. He had asked her to please give him a couple of extra months so that he could continue searching a bit longer for his mother's wedding ring, for that meant a lot to him. He held her in his arms and reassured her of his love and good intentions. The Captain asked her to please be patient about his present line of work, for he was considering his options and would make his decision soon enough, the very moment he returned from Tampa.

Chapter 6
FREAKISH HAPPENINGS ON BOARD

The Captain was a prudent man. For some reason, he thought that he should bring more food on board than usual for the fishing voyage to Tampa. He carried on board cans of food, and also dried salted cod and cured ham, plus plenty of drinking water to keep well hydrated. He also brought along a rifle and bullets, just in case he needed them. Before leaving, he had asked Andy if he wanted to come along, but Andy had matters to tend to in Miami and turned him down politely. The Captain now realized that Andy had been lucky not to have taken part in this voyage, for on his way back home from Tampa, a storm had immobilized the Esperanza, and the boat was now drifting slowly within the Gulf Stream.

The next morning, he woke up quite early. The weather was fine, the breeze from the south gentle, yet strong enough to push the clouds around. He started to get the cabin back in good shape, and while he was busy in his cabin, a gust of wind lifted up a straw hat that one of the tourists had left behind, and it flew clear over the side. It was huge, several feet across. Penny scampered, and jumped over the transom to retrieve the hat, landing in the water next to the hat. It all happened so fast that Penny did not have time to bark. The moment the hat and Penny hit the water, both disappeared under the waves, and did not surface back up. The Captain was looking elsewhere at the time and did not see what had happened right behind him. Only ripples were to be seen on the water's surface.

The Captain noticed Penny's absence and began searching for his puppy. He climbed the short stairs to the deck and did not see Penny up there. He called out the dog's name and did not hear barking. He promised a treat, but the dog seemingly ignored the offer, for there was silence on deck. He looked everywhere in the boat and under the bed, and he did not find the puppy. The Captain was sad and concerned. What could have happened? It sounded outlandish to even consider it, but could it be that a sea bird had swooped down and carried Penny away in its beak and talons? If so, the culprit would have to be a large bird of prey, like an osprey or an American eagle. He knew that ospreys build their nests over water and eat fish, but not more than that. If Penny was not carried away by a bird of prey, then perhaps the puppy had somehow simply fallen overboard and quickly drowned.

Linda and Andy adored Penny and would be saddened by the news. The Captain was also disconsolate, heartbroken, and angry with himself for not having been more aware of the puppy's doings on deck. What would he tell his mother when she asked about the puppy?

Next thing he did was to give undivided attention to the outboard motors, but no matter how hard he tried, he could not get them to start. Yes, he was an expert,

Freakish Happenings on Board

but his expertise had not worked for him this time around. Rather than sulk, he thought breakfast would perk him up. He cut slices of ham, a few of cheese, and put them between two slices of bread for a sandwich, and thoroughly enjoyed eating it. He drank mineral water and started to feel better, and remembered he had cans of food he could open later on in the days ahead. The Captain thought the Gulf Stream current would pick up. He had a good position locator based on the Loran-C that showed longitude and latitude, but it was useless now because the boat had lost all its power with the storm. The boat kept moving north and west at a better pace. With his binoculars, he still could not see the shore from where he was.

The sun set in a peach and orange blaze. The seabirds were colored a pale crimson by the light as they glided over the face of the swells. He was tired and fell asleep with the gentle rocking of the ship. Again, like the night before, that same side of the Esperanza suffered the impact of two blows. He woke up and felt justifiably alarmed. He went on deck and looked out over the waves. He knew that the world's oceans are vast and brimming with latent destructive power. It made sense that the Captain should be alarmed by the collisions. On deck, he looked around and saw nothing unusual that merited his attention. He then looked up to heaven and said a silent prayer asking that his boat be kept safe from wind and waves. He walked down the steps to his cabin, moved to his bedside, sat down, and then, slowly, laid his head on his pillow and tried to return to his dreams.

The following morning, after opening cans, he made his breakfast, nothing very special. He decided to catch fresh fish. The Captain took out a fishing line and hook, baited it with some beef jerky, and cast it overboard. He soon caught a bonito and started to bring it in. A large triangular fin sliced the water. He heard a "whoosh" sound, and the fish and line disappeared into an enormous maw full of sharp teeth shaped like scythes. He shivered. The Captain knew now, without doubt, that a large shark was the sole culprit of the vicious nightly attacks on his boat, and perhaps was to blame for the strange and sudden disappearance of Penny. A new fear was now real to him. What to do? It seemed likely that the shark had been following his boat all along, perhaps upon leaving Tampa's port waters. Because of its dark back, the shark's outline did not stand out from its surroundings, and so, the ancient monster had been unnoticed until now. A few days ago, he had thought of tying a rope around his waist and jumping overboard to inspect the propellers at close range. He'd been lucky, for it would have cost him his life!

.

Chapter 7
MARIO'S PERSONAL EXPERIENCE WITH SHARKS

His surprise at finding out that a huge tiger shark had been following his every move, and had possibly chosen him for his next meal, brought to the Captain's mind much to think about. An incident that had happened to him in Cuba troubled him greatly now.

In his youth, before his friends ever called him "Captain," he was known as Mario Fernandez, for that was his family name. He had an insatiable curiosity about sharks. He learned about sharks by reading publications by the National Geographic Society and by listening to his uncle Carlos Fernandez, a scientist who was rich in information about sharks. Mario learned that they appeared on this planet about four hundred million years ago, earlier than the dinosaurs. Sharks had survived the wholesale extermination of most plants and animals on this planet more than once. These events had occurred at various times in earth's planetary existence.

His uncle told him that although the Cretaceous-Tertiary (C-T) extinction event is the better known because it wiped out the dinosaurs, there were a series of other mass extinction events that had occurred throughout the history of the earth, some even more devastating than the C-T. Mass extinctions are periods in earth's history when abnormally large numbers of species died out simultaneously or within a limited time frame. The most severe occurred at the end of the Permian period, when ninety-six percent of all species perished. This extinction, along with the C-T extinction, constituted two of the five mass extinctions. Each one wiped out at least half of all species. It's known that smaller-scale mass extinctions had also taken place.

In some of the islands in the Pacific and Indian Oceans, sharks are considered to be all-powerful gods. Sharks appeared to Mario to be indestructible beings. Volcanism had not killed the sharks. Asteroid impacts had not, and neither global warming, nor ice ages, nor disease, nor viral cancer, nor pollution, nor infections, nor circulatory diseases, nor the hand of man had managed to wipe out all the sharks. Incredibly, shark wounds heal themselves with unbelievable speed. In the world's oceans, the shark reigns at the top of the food chain, and its only known ocean predators are the orca whales, but not all of them. The great white sharks, for instance, can be killed only by those orcas that belong to a particular pod that had previous experience killing a shark, and only if these experienced killer orcas had taught the maneuver to other members of the orca pod.

Sharks have lived a very long time on planet Earth, more than enough geological time for evolution to happen. This had enabled them to hone their anatomy and their senses to the highest degree. They were now the flawless, consummate predators of mankind in our oceans and seas, and even in rivers and lakes. No matter how enlightened we feel when talking about the great role they play in preserving the health of the oceans by eating the old and the weak fish, people all over the world fear their attacks and won't stay in the water when a lifeguard shouts, "Shark!"

Mario's uncle, Carlos Fernandez, had a Doctorate in Marine Biology. He had taught in many universities and was an expert on sharks. Carlos had written books and articles on these aquatic predators. Many of the articles he wrote had also been published in the National Geographic and in other science publications. Carlos saw in Mario a kindred spirit and would take him along on fishing trips near the fishing port of Cojimar. There, walking along the beach, he would explain about the dead sharks on the beach by indicating their body features and capabilities.

There were sharks on the sand the fishermen had caught earlier. Passersby walking on the beach thought the sharks were already dead, joked about them, and some even kicked them, but many of the sharks were still alive and harbored concealed ferocity. If someone, quite unwittingly, got too close, the sharks would lunge at the legs or feet of passersby with mouths wide open, snapping, and trying to bite their extremities. There was a pervasive fear of a kind of shark that was big and wide and also particularly aggressive. Later on, Mario realized the fishermen were talking about the bull shark and the tiger shark. Many of the aggressive sharks on the beach at Cojimar were tiger sharks.

Because Mario was interested in knowing more about sharks, his uncle had lent him bound, typewritten pages that contained the information on sharks he communicated in his university lectures. He passed on to his nephew all he knew about sharks, a little bit at a time. Once he took him to see the huge bulk of a dead whale shark, more than twenty feet long, caught by fishermen. It was one of the first ever caught worldwide. The crowds surrounding the dead shark were numbered in the hundreds. Mario was amazed.

Some of the deep waters in Cuba are found off its north coast. The port of Cojimar, not far away from Havana, is located in that zone. It is thought that living at such depths may affect the shark's relative size. Other factors, like the pristine condition of the seawater, and the abundance of fish, may also play a greater role in trying to explain why sharks in Cuba seemingly tend to grow larger than in other places.

Mario was a beachgoer in his youth, a competitive swimmer who never ventured beyond where the water starts getting deep. He knew about sharks and how large they grew in Cuba. He was twenty-six years old, and it was a hot, sweltering July at the beach. The water shimmered a liquid silver sheen, and Mario was bored and baking in the sand. That memorable day, his ten-year-old cousin, named Tomas, pleaded to be taken out in Mario's rowboat to fish. They boarded his rowboat and pushed out across a deep lagoon, following the coastline. His cousin's small baited hook sank below the boat's trailing wake. Mario harbored no expectations: a small shrimp on a small hook does not make a tempting bait for much more than very small fish, but he was wrong. The ancient predator is truly "a nose-that-swims."

Suddenly, a huge dorsal fin popped up by the boat's stern where little Tomas sat, oblivious to all but the cool sea breeze. Mario blanched with fear. If the huge shark had rammed the boat, his cousin would have fallen into its jaws! Mario shouted, "Shark! Drop the line, Tomas! Dive into the boat!" Tomas did as told, and the huge fin fully disappeared under the waves. They were terrified.

Mario still had a half hour of rowing to do to reach the pier of their destination. The original plan had been that, on reaching the pier, they would go swimming in that beach, eat something, and start on the return trip. Cousin Tomas refused the return trip and phoned his mother to pick him up. Mario was flustered but not defeated. He continued with the original plan, swam at that beach, ate something, and started on his return trip.

The sun had begun its descent, and the shadows were beginning to lengthen. He was rowing on what seemed to him an endless sea, with no other boats in view, where the sea and the sky appeared to merge and become one. He felt totally alone, strangely apprehensive, but also exhilarated, enjoying the joy and sensation of being alive, adrift and seemingly weightless within a blue-green crystal of seawater. Softly caressed by a cool and gentle breeze, Mario was lost in thought, deep in his reverie, while the rowboat bore him lightly over the blue-green sea.

He heard nothing but the lapping of the waves on the sides of his rowboat, and the sound of wavelets striking the oars. Suddenly he saw, out of the corner of one eye, a large torpedo shape that rocketed under the boat. Mario saw that it was a six-foot-long tiger shark. The shark surfaced, flipped, stared at him, opened its mouth, and showed him all of its sharp teeth, and Mario thought it said to him, "Jump in, the water's fine!" and, "Never mind, I'll catch up with you another time!"

Mario reacted instantly and, with his oars, propelled the boat over the shallower side of the reef, attempting to leave the shark behind. He rowed for a few minutes and turned his head around and saw that the tiger shark was now following his boat. Alarmed, he sought to defend himself and hopefully repel its attacker by wielding, as a baseball bat, the spare oar he always carried in the rowboat. Mario deliberately ceased rowing until the shark caught up to his boat, and then in desperation, he stood up, raised up his oar, and brought it down as hard as he could, raining heavy blows on the shark's head until the shark stopped its attack.

Startled, the shark instantly turned around and frantically swam away from the boat, but its quick retreat lasted only for a few minutes. Mario kept on rowing, turned his head to check on the shark, and saw the dorsal fin again slicing the water, desperately trying to catch up. He changed course, and this time, he rowed his boat over the shallowest part of the reef. As the shark approached, Mario saw that a big wave was bearing down on his rowboat. The wave caught up with the boat and took control, rocketing the rowboat all the way up to its crest. The rowboat rode the wave down and over the reef into the calmer water on the other side. It rode on a cushion of water and foam that passed over the reef with only inches of clearance above the jagged surface of the sharp coral. The shark could not follow. It would have been torn to shreds by the coral had it tried to do so.

When he reached the shallow water on the other side, Mario was rattled, shaking. He thanked God profusely, anchored the boat on the sand flats, and waded ashore. He climbed up on a big promontory, looked out across the reef, and caught a glimpse of a dark fin cleaving the water surface. The shark was on the other side of the reef, swimming at a fast pace, meandering in and out, savagely hunting for Mario's rowboat.

The shark's fruitless attempt to devour Mario had the surprising effect of diminishing its enthusiasm for preying on humans for the time being. Mario was the first human he had tried to attack and consume. The tiger shark was taken aback by this human's strong determination to live and his vigorous counterattack. The shark did not expect a role change: from being the attacker to being the attacked. No other animal or fish had ever defended against its attacks with such strength, courage, and determination. The tiger shark would never, ever forget Mario's face!

One day, many years after the incident between the Captain and the tiger shark, the tiger shark was swimming by one of the new luxury hotels built in Varadero Beach, Cuba, for the enjoyment of vacationing European tourists. The European tourists loved the ambiance the ultra-modern, luxury hotel provided; loved its wonderful food and exotic drinks, its dance music; and most of all, delighted in swimming, sailing, and surfing the clear blue waters of Varadero Beach. One day, the hotel advertised the first of its invitational international competitive races among windsurfers. Some of the best European windsurfers travelled to Cuba and enrolled in the race. The course to follow was marked by red buoys so that the competitors would not stray from the correct path of the race. It was very exciting to watch the windsurfers on their elongated boards as they were pushed ahead by the powerful ocean breezes. They plowed through the waves, lifted up by their beautiful, brilliantly colored sails like a group of colorful butterflies gracefully skimming the top few inches of a turquoise-blue sea.

One of the surfboards unexpectedly received a gust of wind so powerful that it pushed against its sail and took control of the craft, carrying the windsurfer on his board across the line of red buoys and straight out into the open ocean. The windsurfer let go of the sail to come to a full stop, and while trying to lift the sail back to its normal position, a shark jumped up and took a bite, pulling him into the water, and causing deep puncture wounds that bled copious amounts of blood.

The scent of blood in the water summoned three reef sharks and a bull shark to join the first attacker in its assault on the surfer. They formed a ring around the downed windsurfer and pushed in from all directions to further maul him. The windsurfer valiantly tried to defend himself by hitting the sharks with his closed fists and pulling his legs up as far as he could into his body. The vibrations, the sound waves, and the scent of blood pushed out and spread in all directions. Like a dinner bell, the stimuli beckoned the cruising tiger shark. The vibrations impacted the tiger shark's lateral line and brought it right into the middle of the melee.

At the sight of the rushing tiger shark, all the other attacking sharks quickly peeled away, and this particular tiger shark found itself face to face with a bleeding, helpless human in the water. It was a welcome surprise, and nothing could stop him now from continuing the attack. It swum in and took a bite that carved out a huge chunk of flesh from the windsurfer, and the shark descended to the sandy bottom where it consumed most of the windsurfer's body. Following that, it returned to the surface and closed its jaws around the uneaten remains of the windsurfer's body, took them down to the sandy bottom once more, and hastily fed.

At the beach, the spectators alerted the police about the missing windsurfer. An alarm was triggered, and police officers climbed into a coast guard speedboat and rushed out through the waves. They found the missing board floating on the water, with its red sail intact. The police searched all over but did not find even a trace of the windsurfer.

Chapter 8
A HISTORY OF PREDATION

A pregnant female tiger shark arrived in the waters off Cuba's north coast and lingered there, waiting for the signal her body would be sending that she was about to give birth. The shark took shelter in coral reefs and dropped fifty pups from its uterus one day, and because it was famished, she ate some of them. At the same time, with blood in the water, there was a surge in cannibalism. The larger shark pups attacked and consumed some of their smaller brethren in shark frenzies. Afterwards, the pups dispersed in all directions as fast as they could to elude attacks from larger predators and especially from the voracious mother shark.

One particular tiger shark pup showed more pronounced, darker stripes than its brethren and strange markings on its dorsal fin. It was also extremely voracious and aggressive, consuming large quantities of squid and reef fish, especially croakers and red snappers. The shark grew fast, and in a few years had reached a length of six feet. It was still too small to fight the larger sharks for the females, but eventually it reached twenty feet in length, and no other shark could stand against it or be successful with the females while this massive male tiger shark was nearby.

This particular tiger shark normally ranged north into the Gulf of Mexico from its usual habitat in the Cuban coral reefs. It could be found there, in the reefs, and along the coastlines of Florida, and it ranged even as far away as the Marquesas Keys and the fertile grounds of the Dry Tortugas, seeking young sea turtles, small dolphins, and the slow-moving manatees. There are sand banks almost everywhere, and that's where stingrays live; and this tiger shark was especially fond of their flesh.

Its history of predation of humans started in Cuban waters, where it had attacked swimmers and surfers. The second human torn apart and devoured by the shark was a spear fisherman who was also a champion Olympic swimmer. His undoing was a stringer of fish that dangled from his belt as he moved over a reef. The shark came swiftly from behind and below and closed its jaws on the fish and the man. There was no fighting back.

Human prey was much to its liking because they were weak, helpless, terrified, and easy to prey upon. The shark did not hesitate in attacking humans whenever it encountered them. It was on its way to becoming rogue, because it had tasted human flesh more than once and had a predilection for it. The shark also preyed on fish, dolphins, and sea turtles, and fortunately for humans, there are more of them in the ocean than hapless humans.

As the shark neared the port of Tampa, it became aware of a boat leaving the protection of the port and heading out in the direction of the Florida Keys. That boat was the Esperanza. The tiger shark's first instinct was to follow it. It knew from experience that humans were careless about disposing of trash fish, waste food, and fish parts and would simply throw the unwanted fish and food overboard. It considered if it would be worthwhile to follow the boat to its home base, but it saw at the very same moment a bale of sea turtles heading in the direction of the Bahamas and decided to follow them there, for it knew the Bahamas as a place where fish and humans abounded.

The western islands of the Bahamas are located only fifty miles from Florida's east coast. Now in the Bahamas, preceded by an escort of pilot fish, the tiger shark closely followed a sailboat cruising along the island chain. As the shark swam by, its dark top reflected virtually no light, and so, it had remained unseen by the honeymooners. Suddenly, the tiger shark, with a powerful burst of speed, closed in on the sailboat. The honeymooners, totally unaware of the shark's presence, felt a powerful impact on the sailboat's right gunwale that caused the boat to capsize. The distressed couple found themselves in the water. They saw a dark dorsal fin appear, seemingly out of nowhere, slicing the water surface and heading in their direction. They hugged each other and screamed. The incoming dorsal fin was the last image they saw before they were torn apart and devoured.

Ramming was an activity that proved worthwhile for the tiger shark because it succeeded in most cases. The shark also used it to prey on smaller-sized whales and dolphins. Stunned from the impact of the blow and unable to escape or mount a successful defense, the mammals were easy prey.

A VOYAGE FRAUGHT WITH PERIL: THE **CAPTAIN, LINDA** AND THE **TIGER SHARK**

One early afternoon, a lifeguard stood waist deep in the surf and surveyed the scene on the beach. The sun was shining, but clusters of clouds flew in like ships and were soon gone to become rain elsewhere. Light clouds in the sky drifted in and out, and often lingered, providing a temporary measure of shade. He felt relatively safe in the water; it was not too late or too early in the day for him to be particularly concerned about his own safety from shark attacks, and also, the pier was at his back and within swimming distance. The incoming waves pushed him back somewhat and generated soft currents that picked up fine particles of sand. The sand swirled around him and made the surrounding water cloudy and opaque.

He started to swim parallel to the sandy shore, closed his eyes, and propelled himself in cadence with the incoming swells. His swimming abilities were undeniable. He had a well-toned and muscled body, an athlete's body. The lifeguard had rescued many panicked swimmers from harm and knew what to say to calm them down and get them to shore as fast as possible.

He was aware that swimmers, enjoying the waves at sunrise and sunset, were frequent targets of shark attacks. It had actually happened that month, just a few miles down the coast. If he had to give advice about dealing with sharks, he would say to not engage in swimming, skin diving, spear fishing, body surfing, board surfing, paddle boarding, windsurfing, sea-kayaking, and floating on inflatable rafts when away from the safety of land, especially if alone. The lifeguard would not be there at the beach early or late in the day to provide any assistance, and whether he was there or

A History of Predation

not, those activities would ramp up the possibility of drawing in inquisitive sharks.

Without nets, there was no protection against a savage shark attack, and no rescue possible if people were alone by themselves. Humans forgot they were interlopers in the ocean. There is no conflict more menacing, less survivable, than the attack on a helpless human being by a hungry shark.

The lifeguard continued swimming and settled into a comfortable stroke. His arms and legs hit the water hard, setting up a drumming sound that was loud and rhythmic. Far out at sea, the tiger shark received a faint signal, but it was almost a beacon to the incredible senses of the shark. It turned slowly, trying to locate the source. As the tiger shark swam toward the beach, the faint sound waves grew stronger, louder, and more erratic, and the shark made a quick change in direction. Moving closer, now finally beneath its prey, the tiger shark saw the swimmer in full silhouette, etched by sunlight, and it triggered excitement in the shark. The surprise attack on the swimmer was launched with incredible power from behind. The fish had found its human prey.

The tiger shark, with its mouth wide open in mindless savagery, hit one leg, and then the other, slicing below the knees. It was done instinctively to stop its prey from escaping by swimming away. The lifeguard screamed and cried out for help. Everyone around heard the pain and panic in his voice and rushed to help him. Rowboats were untied from the pier and people on the beach crammed into them. When they reached the injured man, he was beyond help. They pulled him out of the water trailing copious amounts of blood and placed him in one of the boats. The tiger shark did not go away but kept circling the boat. Just then they saw, horrified, that the lifeguard had lost both his legs below the knees. He bled to death inside the boat before it could even reach the pier.

The pickings had been good so far, and the shark decided to linger in the Bahamas. It unleashed a wave of attacks that alarmed the tourists and locals and kept them practically glued to the sand and at a safe distance away from the water. The first victim was a paddle boarder. He saw the tiger shark approaching, and thinking he could outswim the shark, he dove from his board into the water, kicking with his feet hard and spasmodically, swimming as fast as his arms and legs would propel him through the waves. The shark caught up with him two body lengths away from the shore and struck him again, and again, savaging the paddle boarder, shredding his limbs, and swimming away from the beach with the paddle boarder in tow before consuming him. Families on the beach saw it happen and were horrified. They covered their children's eyes and screamed in panic.

There was an attack about every two days, and the press faithfully reported each one. One day, as it was cruising nearby, the shark was drawn in by the splashing sounds coming from a pair of surfers who were focused on catching the perfect waves, and unaware that a dark dorsal fin sliced the water a couple of feet away. They suddenly realized their peril but were so frightened at the sight of the shark fin that they lost their balance and tumbled into the crashing wave, landing a few feet away from the waiting shark. One surfer lost his right foot to the shark, and his surfer buddy was never seen again.

A History of Predation

A few days later, by chance, the tiger shark encountered a group of swimmers outfitted in scuba gear, wearing wetsuits, and masks, standing on the sandy bottom. They were tourists enjoying an underwater show staged and led by a couple of men also in scuba gear. Taller than a man in height, a wide steel cage rested on the sand. There was also a small wire cage shaped like a cube that held fish, the very dead fish that tourists would feed to the sharks when it was their turn to do so. About seven reef sharks and a few bull sharks glided around and between them, all part of a spectacle that catered to tourists staying in the big hotels who wanted the thrill of hand-feeding hungry sharks.

It happened that a hungry shark was too eager, too hungry, to wait its turn, and rushed in at top speed with an open mouth, miscalculated, and took both the fish and the tourist's hand in one large bite. There was blood shooting from the tourist's arm, and the water turned red. The sharks went crazy, attacking and trying to bite the tourists. It was pandemonium. The scent and taste of blood in the water, and the powerful sound vibrations, brought in the large tiger shark that was swimming in the vicinity.

It wasted no time, rushed in and swam straight to the injured man, opened its mouth wide, and fit the tourist's torso into its closing jaws. It then swam away with the victim's body protruding half way out of its jaws, the man still very much alive and struggling, his face frozen in terror.

Fortunately for the tourists, a large steel cage was part of the act, and the men in charge of the group maneuvered the tourists into the cage, keeping the snapping sharks at bay. Soon a rescue party arrived at the scene. The hotel's paying customers were brought up to the boat by divers, one on either side, as soon as it was considered safe to swim and carry out the rescue.

In total, the rogue tiger shark had killed or maimed with impunity ten vacationers in a span of three weeks. This fish did not know fear. Its impulse to feed, or to kill, was non-stop and powerful, and it struck again and again. The news of the shark attacks appeared in all the newspapers, and the ensuing panic caused the tourists to stay away from the hotels. The hotels lowered their prices, but that apparently had no effect. The managers then got together and offered a one-hundred-thousand-dollar reward to the person who managed to kill the rogue shark and put an end to its reign of terror. The man-eater could be easily identified by the distinctive dark markings on its body and dorsal fin.

Some people doubt there is such a thing as a rogue shark. One of the better-documented cases to substantiate the proposed theory that a lone shark will occasionally become a confirmed man-eater involved the series of five shark attacks occurring off the New Jersey coast in the summer of 1916. All the attacks took place within a period of two weeks. Four of the five attacks were fatal. When a shark with human remains in its stomach was caught and killed a few days after the last predatory shark attack, there were no more shark attacks reported.

Chapter 9
THE ROGUE SHARK SEARCHES FOR THE ESPERANZA

Having satiated its hunger for the time being, the tiger shark headed due west and approached the US mainland, swimming parallel to the eastern coast of Florida. It was now entering a strong current, warmer than the surrounding waters, the Gulf Stream. The tiger shark resisted its pull, but the powerful current prevailed. The Gulf Stream runs like a mighty river in the ocean, and it swept the tiger shark away from the shallow, familiar coast. The current was miles wide and rich with prey. It carried a wealth of fish, such as tuna, bonito, dolphin, sailfish, and marlin.

The tiger shark, after departing the Bahamas, tried to locate the fishing boat he'd seen leaving Tampa. The shark's experiences with similar boats of that size it had encountered had been that the boats used only a few baited lines to hook fish. Those were the boats that interested the tiger shark, and it had identified the Esperanza that day as a type of fishing boat that merited further investigation.

A VOYAGE FRAUGHT WITH PERIL: THE **CAPTAIN, LINDA** AND THE **TIGER SHARK**

The approach that this tiger shark employed to raid the baited fishing lines on a fishing boat was crucial to the shark's success. It was paramount that its presence went undiscovered by the fishing party on the boat. When fishermen hooked a fish, the tiger shark was able to steal the fish, one after the other, by gently cutting the line with its sharp teeth. There would be no tugging on the line, and no frantic attacks on the hooked fish that could have been considered the work of a hungry shark. The fishermen would quite innocently believe that the hooked fish had been so powerful that it had escaped by its own devices, taking the bait with the hook and line still attached. They would continue fishing until they lost the next hooked fish, and the next one as well, and so on, until the shark's hunger was fully satiated, and it swam away somewhere else. The fishermen on board caught many good fish after that, and this time around they got to keep their catch!

As it continued swimming in the Gulf Stream searching for the Esperanza, the tiger shark had no idea where the boat was. The Esperanza was also caught within the Gulf Stream, in eddies that had slowed down its progress. Some warm water eddies had broken away from the Gulf Stream and drifted into cooler water areas of the ocean. They would confine many fish, and in a way functioned as "fish pens," holding large groups of fish that resisted leaving their preferred water temperatures. The shark was also unaware that the Gulf Stream current would eventually take it right to the boat it was looking for and, further on, would place it in the path of thousands of schooling black tip sharks in their yearly migration. Fortunately for the tiger shark, the tropical storm had left the boat it was searching for, the

The Rogue Shark Searches for the Esperanza

Esperanza, without power and at the mercy of wind and current. It was a favorable turn of events for the shark because the Esperanza was now a slowly drifting target.

Once found, the boat's passengers would not escape the tiger shark's planned attacks. The shark would not hesitate consuming any of the weak, helpless humans it assumed were on board the Esperanza. It knew by experience that black tip sharks were not easy to corral and catch, but humans definitely were, and the shark was looking forward to a preying bonanza.

Drifting on the Gulf Stream, the Esperanza was like a floating reef that provided shade, food, and protection to the fish hiding underneath. There, smaller fish would be preyed upon by the medium-sized-fish, and so on. Perched at the very top of the food chain, the tiger shark would partake of all the fish it wanted at its own leisure. This time, however, it had been seeking human prey.

But, the tiger shark would have to protect the school of fish under the boat from predators like barracudas and other sharks, and there were many of them in these waters. If by chance a human on board should lose its footing and end up in the water, the shark would be right there to attack and devour him or her. It would know what was happening on board the boat Esperanza at all times because the shark gained a clear view of the deck when pushed up by the swells.

All of a sudden, the shark caught up with the Esperanza. It positioned itself facing the boat's stern. A swell pushed the shark high enough to be able to see inside the deck. But, it had seen just one person on board, Mario Fernandez, and a small hairy animal, one that made a lot of noise. The shark had not identified the human on board as the man who had fought against it in

Cuban waters. It now heard a splashing sound coming from the water by the Esperanza, and the shark rushed to the spot, hoping that it belonged to a human who'd fallen overboard.

Instead, he found not a human, but a small furry animal trying to keep its head above water. The shark was upset, frustrated. It had been played for a fool! The human had tricked him with the offering of this pathetic-looking small and hairy animal in his stead, and it had fallen for it. It then took its revenge on the hapless puppy and attacked it with ferocity! Drowning would have been far better for Penny than what actually took place: it was crushed slowly in its jaws and eaten on the spot by the shark. To make matters worse, the slaughter had happened by design just a few feet away from the human, who was totally unaware of the horrible fate suffered by his missing puppy. The next day, the tiger shark swam up on a swell to take a new look at the deck.

Like the day before, it saw only one human on board, Mario Fernandez, but the shark hoped there were other humans on board. To the shark, there was something about this particular human that now triggered a strong response in him. It finally recognized the face, an older face now, which brought to mind memories of a time in Cuba when it had first encountered him. The tiger shark had suffered painful blows from an oar this human had wielded to save himself from being devoured. It had been unable to kill and consume the human that time. The Captain had been lucky to survive that first encounter, but the shark was determined to rewrite the ending in its favor this second time around.

When they'd met, the shark had been smaller and less powerful, and it had not tasted human flesh as yet.

The shark somehow instinctively knew, or rather hoped, that with time they would meet again... and now, they found themselves facing each other once more. The tiger shark considered waiting until the evening hours, when the man would probably be asleep, to test the strength of the hull with a couple of blows. It had done that already the previous night, but the hull had not cracked under the impacts, and the boat had not sunk. It would try again.

The new collisions brought the worried human up on deck. The shark loathed this human and couldn't wait to take its revenge on him. The hatred it felt had been simmering all these years, unabated. The shark had planned other attacks for the following nights to keep the Captain rattled and unbalanced. Deep in its primitive brain festered a mindless hatred and contempt for this wily human, and now it had surfaced full force, an irrepressible, all-consuming malevolence.

Chapter 10
HIS DAILY LIFE ON BOARD / MAKES HIS DECISION

The day is fresh, barely new, yet the Captain felt it to be already spent, fully worn out. It had a lot to do with his present state of mind. The passing days fell heavily upon him. He suffered one endless gloomy day after another in labored succession, not just because the days had been dark and stormy, but simply because he was in the grip of a powerful feeling of melancholy. The Captain watched the days succeed each other lazily, devoid of purpose, like leaves that failed to carry out their daily mission of photosynthesis and had no other plan than to drop and cover the ground in a carpet of brown. The Captain missed Linda by his side. In his thoughts and dreams, he talked to her almost every night.

Storms were accompanied by spectacular displays of lightning, and then the sky lit up like a Christmas tree. The Gulf Stream waters generated their own microclimate and also spawned distinct areas of low pressure that became a breeding ground for many of the severe storms impacting people living on the

Eastern Seaboard. Whenever the Gulf Stream current flowed against a strong opposing wind, waves built up quickly, becoming steeper and more dangerous than under normal conditions, and it all happened in a very short span of time.

Something else about the Gulf Stream that the Captain had not heard before, but was experiencing now, had to do with the presence of eddies moving within the main current. An eddy is a circular current of water that moves counter to a main current, causing a small whirlpool to form. Getting caught in the wrong side of an eddy slowed a boat to a great degree. Some eddies, like the one by the Esperanza, were circular water currents that did not reach deep below the surface and presented no danger to boats, but they did affect the forward movement of the boat.

Flying fish chased by predators leapt out of the water, but regardless of the length of their flights, many did not escape predation either from below by predator fish or from above by hungry sea birds. Way above the Esperanza, all kinds of seabirds crisscrossed the sky and at times lingered, circling the boat. The play of light and shadow created a web of illusions. Clouds became strange animals, and a few moments later dissolved back into clouds, or became fluffy sea monsters, or jolly snowmen. There were mirages that were pleasing, totally harmless, and others that occasionally led sailors to their demise, and then, their boats were never found.

All around him was a hostile wilderness, a dynamic, indifferent world. The ocean seemed to be an uncontrollable ancient deity, more like Poseidon, the Greek's jealous and vindictive god of the sea. The ocean, all fishermen believed, had its many moods. Sometimes the ocean was even tempered (when the sun was shining and the waves were manageable), and sometimes it was hostile and furious (a Poseidon, guilty of having sent that destructive tropical squall his way). The ocean was powerful beyond measure, and at times, the sheer enormity of its dominion over the lives on its waters and under the waves made the Captain feel helpless and abandoned by his God.

THE LEATHERBACK TURTLE

But thankfully, the Captain was not totally alone on his boat. He had seen a medium-sized leatherback turtle close by the boat's stern. Impulsively, he had cast a net over it, and had brought it on board. The Captain owned a large plastic wading pool that was perfect for holding the leatherback turtle. He always kept the wading pool inside the boat and would drag it out and fill it with water whenever his customers got back on board after swimming in the Florida beaches. That way, he thought, they could wash off the sand that stuck to their feet and legs and keep the deck as clean as it could be.

The Captain filled the wading pool with cool seawater, placed the leatherback turtle inside, and fed it a few jellyfish. He believed the sea turtle was female and that it had earlier mated in the ocean and carried inside her the eggs that would eventually be buried at a nearby sandy beach. It was a middle-sized sea turtle, and he believed its size meant that it was not old, but middle-aged. He surmised that female leatherback turtles were more cautious than the males because it was their very important role to assume all of the responsibility for the safe keeping of the embryo eggs of the next generation of sea turtles.

He proposed to no one in particular, expecting no reply, "Who would not love an animal that ate mostly stinging jellyfish?" Leatherback turtles are known to devour jellyfish starting from the tentacles up, as if they were eating spaghetti, with eyes closed, and using the flippers to protect its head. The Captain was a happy man now. He believed that the leatherback turtle was a special gift from the waves that had found its way to him through the foam and the tangling seaweed and had reached his boat unscathed. He was fishing in his mind for a good feminine name for the leatherback turtle, but found no name suitable enough for it, and gave up the search.

The leatherback turtle had not been captured to become the Captain's next meal. Oh no! It was brought on board to become, instead, the Captain's daily companion. The Captain knew something about the leatherback turtles. His uncle had told him that they had been around for more than 150 million years and survived the dinosaur extinction. It's known that the leatherback turtles, when fully grown, may reach a length of six feet, and live to be thirty to sixty years old. Leatherback turtles differ from other sea turtles in that they lack a hard shell or scales. Each leatherback turtle is covered with a firm, protective, rubbery skin that allows it to tolerate cold water. Luckily, the leatherback turtle was able to fit nicely within the confines of the wading pool.

In the US, it nests in Southeast Florida, Puerto Rico, and the US Virgin Islands. Their survival is at stake, threatened by rapacious fishermen catching them with nets, or by villagers digging up their eggs to eat or sell.

A major problem is predation of baby sea turtles. If a nest has one hundred hatchlings, about ninety-five will make it to the water if they are born during the night, but if they are born during the day, they won't survive predation.

The leatherback turtles eat mostly jellyfish, but also some sea grass, fish, and crustaceans. The Captain thought that not many sea creatures were nicer and less threatening than the leatherback turtles, and that is why he thought they'd be good and loyal friends. And yet, they were not defenseless in the ocean. Each adult leatherback turtle aggressively protected itself from predators with mixed results. A fisherman friend told the Captain once that he had observed a leatherback turtle chase a shark that had tried to bite it, and failing to reach the shark, it reacted angrily by focusing its aggression on his friend's boat.

With Penny gone, the presence of the leatherback turtle allowed the Captain to overcome the terror of extreme loneliness, and the hopelessness of living day-to-day trapped and drifting in a boat that headed nowhere he knew or wanted. He craved company, needed a friend. He decided to put into words all of his doubts, concerns, and expectations of rescue to share later with the leatherback turtle. The Captain was happy that there was another living being on board who would listen to his remarks and then gaze at him with its large soft brown eyes, as if it had understood his every word and was in total agreement. He had no further expectations of the leatherback turtle's role in his boat beyond becoming his listener.

For these reasons, the Captain saw the leatherback turtle as a gift. It was God's way of saying He cared.

A VOYAGE FRAUGHT WITH PERIL: THE **CAPTAIN, LINDA** AND THE **TIGER SHARK**

The Captain found a significant measure of relief from his despondency while in the company of the leatherback turtle. Finally, his prayers were answered because there was someone on board now who would listen to his every word and help make his lonely predicament somewhat bearable!

Poetry books that Linda gifted him, he read from cover to cover, and following her advice, he would recite each poem aloud. She had told him that by reading aloud, he would best decipher the poem's meaning. He owned lots of books and kept them in a bookcase in his cabin. They were kept there for the use of his paying customers. The books were very appropriate to his present situation, and all had something to do with the ocean. He went downstairs to his chamber and collected a few books that he thought he'd enjoy reading for the first time, or re-reading. He would follow Linda's advice and read the books aloud. He had no other competing uses of his time

Daily, the Captain would translate his innermost feelings into words. He spoke loudly, but softly, not only because of Linda's advice, but also because he thought his voice would soothe the captive sea turtle. He realized that it was strange for him to be doing something as crazy as that, and he wondered if he was losing his mind. To him, it didn't matter that his guest was a leatherback turtle and not a human being. Being alone in the open ocean often makes the human mind dispense with some of the rules of logic and other niceties, and then, it is prone to accept as ordinary what is, under more normal conditions, extraordinary. This was now true for the Captain.

His Daily Life on Board /Makes his Decision

He thought there was not much difference between him and the leatherback turtle within the confines of his boat's deck. The deck was too small a piece of the universe to worry about. No one would ever know how he, personally, had coped with loneliness during this voyage, or perceive that his captive leatherback turtle had become the perfect listener of anything he wished to share. He thought of himself and the leatherback turtle as fellow travelers trapped in a floating wooden cage and drifting on the Gulf Stream. Luckily, that "cage," the Esperanza, protected them from the elements and from the hungry predators of the deep.

He selected books to read during the coming leisure hours, but only chose those that had something to do with the ocean, and perhaps something instructive. Sitting on deck, next to the wading pool where the leatherback turtle now lived, he started reading aloud from a notebook he owned where he had written about his adventures as a fisherman in Cuba. It told of the many dangers he had faced from sea predators that included not only the stingrays and toothy barracudas, but also the cunning and ferocious sharks. As he talked, he saw that the leatherback turtle had moved to the edge of the wading pool closest to the Captain and was gazing at him with those large and mournful brown eyes. The Captain believed, as much as he could tell by the leatherback turtle's actions and expression, that the leatherback had understood him, and loved the stories!

The joys of companionship were unending, and he savored them fully. Having a good friend close by awakened his thirst for further knowledge, especially about survival in the ocean. No, he was not losing his mind today, nor in the coming weeks. He told himself it was simply a game. He was just letting his imagination run free, squeezing every last drop of joy provided by the sea turtle's presence after so many barren weeks of loneliness. He knew it would all pass eventually, for nothing in life is forever, but he would enjoy the ride while it lasted, all the way to its end.

The Captain began to read to the leatherback turtle in a loud but soothing voice. He started with the book written by Kevin Walker titled *Free Willy*. He told the leatherback turtle about an eleven-year-old boy who was trying to find a way to free his new friend, a seven-thousand-pound killer whale, from a miserable existence as the star attraction of an amusement park. About a quarter of the way through it, he turned his head and saw that the leatherback turtle had retreated to the corner of the wading pool farthest away from him, and that it fully avoided eye contact.

The Captain had no idea why the leatherback turtle reacted that way. He asked himself, "Could it be that it was hungry?" He then looked inside the wading pool and saw that there were still crustaceans that were uneaten, and jellyfish still floated in the water, confirming that the leatherback turtle was definitely not hungry. It dawned on the Captain that perhaps the reason for the leatherback turtle's strange behavior might be that the story featured a killer whale, and the leatherback turtle felt threatened by hearing about this predator that could easily make a meal of it. That the leatherback turtle had recoiled in fear now made sense: it was just too scary a story for the sea turtle. It had been a big mistake, his mistake!

In his strange new frame of mind, he thought anything was possible. Maybe his leatherback turtle friend

His Daily Life on Board /Makes his Decision

was different than the others, had a better brain, and was somehow able to react to his stories. The Captain knew he could readily tell which stories frightened the leatherback turtle and which didn't. He tried to reassure the leatherback turtle in a very soothing tone of voice that killer whales (orcas) are not commonly found in tropical waters (although, to be totally honest, he knew they have the ability to do so). The Captain thought that continuing his loud narration about such a frightful predator as a killer whale could move the leatherback turtle to go on a hunger strike and stop eating to show its distress. Or, it would try to commit suicide by jumping out of the wading pool and onto the scorching hot deck. The Captain didn't want that to happen. He did not want to lose his listener friend, so he abruptly stopped narrating the story.

He reflected on what he had seen: aside from the scary orca in the *Free Willy* story, he thought something else had frightened the leatherback turtle. What could it be? Did it have anything to do with him? The Captain wondered if the leatherback turtle believed that he was a possible threat because he was the fisherman who had snatched it out of the water. The leatherback turtle also may have thought the Captain had relatives nearby who were rogue fishermen and preyed on sea turtles, and that possibility may have added even more fuel to its panic!

The Captain quickly reassured his listener, in a mild tone of voice, that it was totally safe with him, and safe in his boat always. He further explained that relatives of his were good and honest Cuban fishermen who made a living catching only fish and were not in the habit of netting sea turtles nor stealing their eggs. In addition, his relatives lived in far-away Cuba and would not be found on the Gulf Stream. In a very dramatic gesture, he put his right hand over his own heart and swore that he never would betray their friendship. The leatherback turtle then looked at him with its large, soulful brown eyes and moved to the edge of the wading pool closest to the Captain, and the Captain thought they had just reached a very deep level of mutual understanding, and smiled.

That said, he reached for an illustrated book about *Popeye the Sailor Man*. He read aloud about Popeye, and his skinny girlfriend Olive, and asked himself how it was possible that Popeye could subsist, and actually thrive, by eating just canned spinach! He showed the leatherback turtle a page of the book he was reading that held a color illustration of Popeye in his sailor suit holding an open can of green spinach. For the Captain, a daily diet of canned spinach was definitely gross and out of the question, but maybe not so for the leatherback turtle because it probably enjoyed eating some green seaweed once in a while.

The Captain planned to introduce a bit of culture into his reading by sharing a masterpiece of ancient literature with the leatherback turtle. He read a classical story titled *The Odyssey* by Homer, the ancient Greek writer. Homer had written about another famous sailor, the shipwrecked Greek hero Ulysses. Ulysses had spent ten years of his life attempting to return to his homeland of Ithaca by sailing from the conquered city of Troy. The Captain had read aloud most of the story, but had carefully abstained from narrating the passages about the bloody massacre of the suitors. Homer's story narrated that Ulysses had killed all of his wife's suitors (about 108) in a single day with his arrows and, aided by his own son, had regained the throne and the love of his faithful wife, Penelope. The Captain somehow knew that his friend, the leatherback turtle, would have been horrified had it heard about the bloody massacre. He had come to believe that his leatherback turtle friend had a soft heart and was fully against cruelty and violence in all of its many forms.

He wondered whether the leatherback turtle had a mate, and how they had both met in the immensity of the ocean, and whether it mated for life. He had many more questions to ask the leatherback turtle: Had the leatherback turtle previously given birth to baby turtles? Also: Did the leatherback turtle love its mate as much as he loved Linda? He was going to pose the questions to the leatherback turtle, but then remembered that Linda had once said that, as a general rule of courtesy and good breeding, it was rude and insulting to ask such personal questions of a new friend (or of any friend for that matter). In addition, the leatherback turtle had never met Linda, so how could there be a true assessment or comparison between their two sweethearts? Instead, he thought he'd narrate the story of the exciting voyages and fantastic adventures of *Sinbad the Sailor*. Perhaps the leatherback turtle had swum in one of the seven seas that Sinbad had fully explored, like the Arabian Sea.

The leatherback turtle was truly his captive audience. For the following morning, he planned to read aloud the story of *Robinson Crusoe*. He was certain that the leatherback turtle had an affinity for islands, most sea turtles do, and the Captain thought it would enjoy the story. He was doing fine in his narration, but the Captain stopped when it occurred to him that it was possible that Crusoe had eaten lots of sea turtles and sea turtle eggs in his lonely island, and possibly his friend, the cannibal, had also done so. (Heaven knows if there had been humans on the cannibal's menu!) This time, however, the Captain continued his narration in hopes that his friend had been fully distracted by the squawking of the seagulls above and was not at all offended by what it had heard so far.

His heart was full of love for his leatherback turtle friend. It had proven to be a good daily companion and a good friend and listener, and he promised that if he survived the voyage he'd volunteer to go to Costa Rica for a whole month. There, he would help sea turtle conservation by guiding the newly hatched baby sea turtles to the surf, and by protecting them from imminent destruction by shooing away the seagulls and other killer seabirds. He would also stop the crabs from capturing the baby sea turtles and despicably dragging them into their holes in the sand to devour them later on. He made an exception concerning jaguars, the worst of Costa Rican nightly predators. He wanted nothing to do with the big cats. He wanted to help, but not to risk his life in the process. The Captain then told his friend, the leatherback turtle, as diplomatically as he could, that he did not want to die confronting a murderous jaguar. He had too much joy and happiness to live for, now and in the near future, to put all of it at risk.

THE CAPTAIN PLANS TO CONFRONT THE SHARK

His mind now drifted away from the leatherback turtle and turned inwards. He realized how dire his chances of survival were in his present situation. He was nearing a moment of reckoning where his life would be at stake, for he knew he would be facing the tiger shark in a mortal encounter, a duel on the Gulf Stream whose outcome was uncertain.

He still had a lot of history to create ahead of him, and a lot of living yet to do as a young adult now in his mid-thirties. He had plans for the future: he would surely expand his marine engine repair business. Also, he had met a wonderful young lady and fervently wished that at the end of the upcoming battle with the shark, he'd still be alive to marry her. These thoughts pushed his mind away from loneliness and into full survival mode.

They say that when humans are about to die, they watch their entire lives projected in their minds as on a screen, covering all the precious moments from birth until the present. At the time of his exodus from Cuba, he knew nothing about America except what he had heard said: "That the US is the home of liberty and promise." He had found that to be true, at least for him.

He remembered, as if it had just happened, that day when he said goodbye to his mother. She had been praying for weeks at her church for a miracle, one that would stop her favorite son from migrating to the United States. Her prayers, however, had not changed his mind. A day before his flight, Esperanza took him to her flower garden and said, "Mario, I love you very much. I have a very special wedding gift for you. It is the most valuable thing I own." Then, she raised her hand up to her chest and pulled her wedding ring off her finger and gave it to Mario. She told him, "This wedding ring has been handed down through the years to a Fernandez bride. I want you to take it with you, son, and when you fall in love with a special young lady, one who loves you with a love that is right and true, to present it to her as your engagement ring. When she wears it on her finger, which should be every day, I pray that it will remind you of me." That said, Esperanza kissed her son and quickly left. She did not want Mario to see her crying.

His mind relived the scene of his arrival in Miami. He was alone and in need then, but ultimately he had succeeded. He was proud of that and soon applied the learned skills and mechanical knowledge to his work at various marinas. He was making a name for himself. Would all that go down the drain? The Captain's ultimate goal at this point in his life is to marry Linda, be able to make a comfortable living for his family and also to be able to pay for his children's education. The rest is sure to come. Who knows what the future holds for him, for all of us? He also knows there will be no future for him if he does not survive. Of this he was certain: he would survive! He'd lost his old Cuban family, but he and Linda would start a new one. He would make it happen sooner or later!

When he lost the bonito to the shark, the Captain was able to take a good look at the predator. It was a large shark, close to twenty feet in length. He recognized it by its sides, the stripes running down from the top of its body, like those on a tiger. It was a tiger shark, a nightmare come to life. He was not ignorant about the shark's aggressive nature, its blatant ferocity. He had also read that tiger sharks are second only to great white sharks in the number of reported attacks on humans, and as far as it was concerned, everything in the water was edible.

The warmer waters of the Gulf Stream were an ideal home for the tiger shark. This shark was not a gourmet.

His Daily Life on Board /Makes his Decision

Its menu consisted of just about anything that finds its way into the ocean. It will gobble up a solid object as quickly as it will swallow a dead animal. The shark would have no qualms about eating humans, even preferring them as prey.

It was now sunset, and the sky was clear, the air blue and luminous, with little wind. The western sky was streaked in yellow and pink. His boat Esperanza looked like it had been painted in sunset colors, bathed in soft colored lights. A light mist enveloped the boat, and the moon was not clearly visible. The night was untroubled by impacts on the boat, and he slept well. When the Captain got up and went on deck the next morning, he found much to worry about: a wing of the propeller had been sliced off, and he could see bite marks all along the metal arms that held the propellers. In his heart, he felt a growing feeling of helplessness, of despair, but he fought it and did not let it take full command.

Situated on the eastern side of the Gulf Stream, in deep seas as close as sixty miles from shore, cold water eddies interacted with warm Gulf Stream water, creating a fishing frenzy second to none. Plankton and baitfish gathered in these eddies, providing an endless food source for tuna and other game fish. The Esperanza was now parked at the edges of this fish bonanza!

The following morning, he was standing on the deck, drinking his coffee and leaning against the outboard motors by the boat's stern, when he felt a powerful impact on the side of the deck where he stood, a blow meant to make him lose his balance and tumble overboard. Hidden by the waves, the tiger shark had been aware of his movements on deck all along. It had been increasing the frequency and intensity of its attacks on the Captain and his boat, Esperanza. The Captain realized that the shark's predatory brain seemed bent on destroying the boat and making a meal of him!

He had read that a ship in the Pacific Ocean had sustained damage when a group of large tiger sharks began ramming the vessel. The next morning, one of them returned and rammed the boat again. Passengers were incredibly lucky that their ship's hull had been strong enough to withstand the onslaught.

In spite of the damage wrought by the tiger shark, his outboard motors were not damaged enough to be beyond repair. He gave thanks to God for that, but he still was unable to re-start them. The boat moved with the Gulf Stream, drifting much faster now. He remembered the Gulf Stream gets closest to land when it passes by the state of Florida. Alarmed by the successive attacks by the tiger shark, the Captain was planning not to spend another night on the boat!

He thought about God and hoped He would be in his corner and watching benevolently over his life. He wondered if God had ever been on the side of the shark. It was a troubling thought, worrisome because millions of men and women throughout history were eaten or mutilated by sharks when their boats floundered in angry seas and their bodies were never found. At that point, he quit his musings because they were not inspirational or hopeful. They were having the opposite effect.

The Captain thought that the tiger shark had fully revealed its intent to capsize the Esperanza and devour him. He asked himself, "Was it revenge?" The Captain remembered that the shark that had stolen his "bonito" in these Gulf Stream waters, showed peculiar dark markings on its dorsal fin, and the markings were identical to those on the tiger shark that had attacked him in Cuban waters years ago, when it was about six feet long.

That time, the Captain, in an act of self-preservation, had forcibly struck the attacking shark's head more than once with one of his oars. He found it logical to assume that the tiger shark had nursed a desire for murderous revenge during all the intervening years, and the Captain thought its revenge would not be postponed much longer.

The Captain heard a couple of shots and looked around his boat and out toward the east and saw what looked like a small ocean fishing boat approaching. It measured about twenty-six feet in length and was built to handle the open ocean and catch albacore tuna and other game fish by trolling. He reached for his binoculars and saw two fishermen on board and also a few albacore tuna inside the boat. The boat approached, and as it neared, one of the men asked, shouting, if he needed some help. The Captain was overjoyed! His prayers had been answered! He shouted back, "Yes!" The fishing boat then advanced slowly toward the Esperanza. At that same moment, he saw with his binoculars that the twenty-foot-long tiger shark was circling the fishing boat and ramming its sides, keeping it away from the Esperanza.

The two fishermen on board, in spite of their good intentions to rescue the Captain, could not afford capsizing their fishing boat in such perilous waters and fighting this super predator, an aggressive tiger shark. They quickly realized that the tiger shark was almost as large as their ship! They had no rifles on board, and so, they rapidly backed their boat away from the

A VOYAGE FRAUGHT WITH PERIL: THE **CAPTAIN, LINDA** AND THE **TIGER SHARK**

Captain, turned the boat around, and accelerating, left the Esperanza behind. It was evident that the tiger shark had claimed the Captain as its prize and would not allow anything, or anyone, to come between it and its prey.
.

Chapter 11
DUEL ON THE GULF STREAM

After the sad incident of his aborted rescue attempt, the Captain noticed that the eddy holding the Esperanza had gradually drifted towards the western edge of the Gulf Stream. The Captain's binoculars now revealed that he was navigating very close to land. With binoculars, he could see the coastline from the boat when it approached within seven miles of it. The Captain saw a line of beaches stretching out on the horizon. From his maps, he could tell he was at the approximate spot where the Gulf Stream runs closest to the Florida coast. It was raining off and on, but the rain had stopped, and the sky suddenly cleared. The sea was calm. The sun spread its wealth all around, and its rays made the water surface glisten. Flying fish took off from the depths and flew through the air, landing on the Esperanza's deck with a thud, and thankfully, the Captain's spirits were buoyed up!

The Captain decided the time had come to release his good friend, the leatherback turtle, from the wading pool on the boat's deck. He was sad to let his friend and companion go. He grabbed the turtle by the edges of its shell, lifted it carefully, and slowly let it slip into the water by the ship's stern. The Captain turned around and was heading to his cabin when he heard a commotion in the water behind him. He moved toward the sound and saw that the tiger shark was attacking the leatherback turtle, and had already bitten off its head and shredded its flippers. It had happened so fast!

Within a span of minutes, he saw the tiger shark crush the leatherback turtle's leather carapace between its powerful jaws. There was dark red blood everywhere! The tiger shark devoured what was left of the leatherback turtle. Scraps and shredded flesh were left floating on the water surface, food for the pilot fish and remoras. The Captain saw that this large tiger shark was the same one that had chased his rowboat unsuccessfully in Cuban waters years ago. He was upset about losing his friend, the leatherback turtle, in such a savagely violent way. He believed that by killing and eating the leatherback turtle, the tiger shark was sending him an additional personal message, issuing a challenge. The message was obvious: "The Captain would suffer the same fate as the leatherback turtle!"

The Captain hatched his action plan. He would lure the tiger shark closer to the boat and try to shoot it using a high power sniper rifle he owned and had brought along just in case. The "just in case" was here and now. The rifle had a very good scope. On land, he often trained with it and paid for target practice at a club near where he lived. It was said that he was a great rifleman, a crack shot.

He inspected his provisions, trying to find some food that he could use as bait that would lure the tiger shark closer to the boat. He had brought along a large piece of salted cod, and he hoped it would make a tempting morsel when dropped in the water next to the boat. The Captain feared that if the tiger shark continued its attacks, the boat's hull would surely leak. It was now or never.

He took a length of chain and placed a shark hook at its end, buried within a slab of cod. He tied a rope to the chain, and the rope to the boat. The Captain cast the rope with the attached floater overboard and waited. Next, he picked up his rifle and made himself ready to fire. He did not have long to wait. A dark, triangular fin sliced the water surface. The tiger shark swam swiftly toward the bait, opened fully its formidable jaws, and with a gulp, swallowed the bait.

The Captain waited a short time to ensure the hook had been swallowed, and pulled down hard on the chain, setting the hook and bringing the hooked tiger shark closer. Next, he fired two shots that hit the tiger shark's sides. The bullets slowed it somewhat, and it fixed its eyes on the Captain, seemingly taking measure of its enemy.

He could be wrong, but he thought that if a shark is capable of feeling hate, then it was pure hate what the Captain saw in its eyes. The tiger shark's eyes were aimed at the Captain, and they were dull and black, funerary eyes, with no hint of emotion inside. Suddenly, the tiger shark submerged and swam straight toward where he was standing. The Captain raised his rifle, aimed through its scope, waited until the shark's head broke the water surface, and shot two bullets into the tiger shark's head. The bullets seemed to stop the shark in its charge because, afterward, it did not move at all.

A VOYAGE FRAUGHT WITH PERIL: THE **CAPTAIN, LINDA** AND THE **TIGER SHARK**

The Captain thought he now had a good chance to make a safe getaway. He lowered the dinghy to the water, jumped in, and pushed on the starter button. The motor roared with unrestrained power and the dinghy took off like a tornado, sprinting for the sandy shore through a vast chaos of unrelenting waves. The tiger shark was not dead. It was merely dazed, but not for long. The tiger shark heard the motor roar to life, and the sound brought it out of its stupor. It pulled hard against the rope that tied the hook to the boat and freed itself. Its tail struck the water and forcibly swung from side to side. Its whole body shuddered, and the murderous fish became like a torpedo aimed at the escaping dinghy.

Chapter 12
THE GETAWAY

It was still light, and from the west, the sun's rays spread out from behind the massed clouds. The moon climbed higher in the eastern sky, slowly becoming the color of polished silver. The Captain turned around and saw that the tiger shark had taken off in rabid pursuit of the dinghy. The dinghy was ahead, and the tiger shark put all of its energy to the task of catching up. The Captain turned his head and looked back and saw the dark shape of the shark as it raced toward the dinghy. He was amazed that after taking four bullets the tiger shark could still go after him with such force. Fortunately for the Captain, the sandy bottom kept getting shallower and shallower.

It was the beginning of low tide, and the water began to drain out of the sand flats. The dinghy kept on racing toward the beach. When the Captain saw the bottom of the dinghy almost touching the sandy bottom, he pulled on the chain that lifted the motor higher and was able to coast, borne on a cushion of water, silt, and sand, practically all the way to the shore.

Meanwhile, the tiger shark, now much closer to making contact with the dinghy, found itself with its bulk touching the sandy bottom. A tiger shark can only sustain its incredible high speeds for a few seconds, and as it tired, it became slower moving. It forcibly swatted the waves with its tail to free itself from the sand, but only managed to dig a deeper hole where it then lay, exhausted. The ebb tide was now in full force, and the water under the tiger shark began to rapidly recede to the depths. The tiger shark was stranded. The water drained away faster and faster, and soon the tiger shark's body lay exposed on the sand flats. The tiger shark could not breathe at all through its gills and collapsed on the wet sand.

The Captain had just enough energy left in him to get out of the dinghy. It was now dark. He dropped anchor so the dinghy would not move during the night. He was not concerned about anchoring his dinghy there because he was very much exhausted physically and emotionally, and there were other boats anchored there. He did not know what had happened to the tiger shark. The Captain took a blanket from the dinghy, dragged himself to the sandy shore and fell asleep on the sand. While he slept, darkness seeped into his mind, clouding, shrouding some of his lifelong memories. He slept soundly the entire night. In the morning, he heard voices, stood up, looked around, and saw a group of people out on the sand flats, all milling around the body of a huge dead tiger shark.

The gulls were sitting on the shark and striking it with their beaks. People in swimsuits were all around, taking photos and alerting the towns' local newspapers of the big news: a huge tiger shark found dead on the

The Getaway

sand flats! The Captain looked around and saw in the distance what seemed like an inlet. He thought he was standing on one of the extensive beaches north of Boca Raton, for the Gulf Stream current passed closest to land around there.

The local newspapers carried photos of the dead tiger shark, and the photos featured prominently on the front page. The text below the photograph revealed a surprising mystery: the tiger shark had been shot four times at close range with a high-power rifle. Four bullets were extracted. Who shot the shark? Where was the shooter?

Chapter 13
A NEW LIFE

The Captain had been under intense emotional and physical stress, having experienced a series of traumatic events that had left a lasting impression on his psyche. It's known that intense physical, mental, and emotional trauma may affect a person's memory. The Captain had withstood in succession a violent tropical storm, the travails of a solo voyage adrift in the fast-moving Gulf Stream, outboard engines that failed to work, and last but not least, persistent attacks from a twenty-foot-long tiger shark, aiming to sink his vessel and make a meal of him.

Memory loss is a natural survivor skill and defense mechanism humans are blessed with to protect themselves from major psychological damage. Persons will often suppress memories of a traumatic event until they are able to fully handle them. Recovering from a traumatic experience is possible. One good thing was that the trauma did not affect the Captain's ability to function normally on his own.

He awoke the following morning feeling strange and knew that something was amiss. He could not remember important facts concerning his identity, like his name, his home address, also the names of loved ones, the places where he had lived before, and where he was now. Fortunately, his memory loss had been only partial and very selective. He thought that maybe he had been a passenger on board a ship that capsized offshore. He realized, however, that although he had suffered some memory losses, he still recalled some of his personal information.

He knew that he owned a dinghy, but not how he came to own it. He knew that he had hidden cash in the dinghy. He also knew that boats were very important to him, and that he could make a living by repairing them and their engines. The Captain realized he needed most of everything: new lodgings, food, and clothing. Foremost, he needed a job, preferably one that involved boat engines. With so many beaches and so many boats around, there had to be marinas nearby. So, he looked for a marina that could use his expertise. He knew marinas invariably used people like him, people with skills in fixing boats and engines. Fortunately, there were several marinas, and he was hired right away. The marina he now worked for helped in giving him an official identity to secure a new social security card. He asked to be paid in cash, off the books, and because the need for his services was so great, management acquiesced. He further asked permission to keep his dinghy moored by their pier, and they also agreed to that.

He walked along the beach searching for his dinghy. The Captain found it anchored where he thought he had left it. The dead shark was nearby, and the Captain wondered if he had actually killed it. He could not remember doing that and had also lost other personal

A New Life

details of his past. His wallet with his driver's license had been left behind on the Esperanza in his frantic escape. Curiously enough, he knew his name was Mario but did not remember his last name. He needed one. The Captain picked "Rodriguez" as his last name. The new last name had a certain ring to it that he liked. He boarded his dinghy and retrieved cash he had hidden inside for an emergency, plus a wedding ring. He didn't know why he was carrying a wedding ring in the dinghy. Next, he passed by a retail clothing store and bought a pair of pants and three shirts, some underwear, socks, shoes, and a light all-weather jacket. He looked for a place to stay, preferably a room in a boarding house close to the beach from which he could walk to work. He searched for one that would serve meals to guests at a communal table on schedule, and found it. The boarding house address was the one he would provide for a new driver's license.

Chapter 14
LIFE IN HIS NEW HOME

A month and a half had passed since his arrival in this seaside village he now called home. He loved the place and made a lot of friends at the boarding house, at the marina, and at a restaurant-bar he frequented. There was even a young lady who worked there who was quite interested in dating the Captain, but he knew deep inside that there was another lady, one he treasured, who was the love of his life. He did not know her identity yet but hoped he would be able to recognize her if ever they met again.

The quality of his work as a marine mechanic was superb, exceptional. In a way, he became once more like an itinerant mechanic, selling his expertise from marina to marina, fixing boats and engines and making some money. His reputation transcended his new home. He was so incredibly good at fixing boat engines that his clients nicknamed him "Magician" because they thought he could do magic in fixing any marine engine. Friends told him he had a rare gift, for they saw clients come in to see him with their boats from as far away as New Orleans.

One day, Florida's leading newspaper reported that the Captain's boat, the Esperanza, was found wedged between two huge boulders off the coast of Iceland. Marine experts speculated that it was carried north by the Gulf Stream to the place it was found, minus passengers. It had been battered, but the hull was intact, with no leaks. His wallet and driver's license were found inside the Esperanza, together with all his food provisions. They dug out from its hull teeth from a tiger shark. The dinghy was missing. After hearing the news, some people concluded that the Captain had lost his life.

Other friends, however, were heartened by the fact that the Captain's precious dinghy was not found, which suggested that perhaps the Captain was able to escape a cruel death. Also, the hull had held, and no leaks were found.

Andy thought that he should fly to Iceland to retrieve the boat and navigate it back home. He knew in his heart that the Captain was alive, and that he would be pleased to have the boat back. He brought with him, to show the Icelandic government, an affidavit affirming the Esperanza was registered in Andy's and the Captain's names. In addition, Andy brought to the officials the documents they had requested. He further backed up his claim with photos of the Captain and himself steering the boat and taking tourists out. Iceland released the boat to Andy right away, and he navigated it back home.

NEW DEVELOPMENTS

Meanwhile, Linda's parents, the Smiths, wasted no time in continuing their attempts to convince Linda to return home. This time, they brought along

Life in his New Home

Linda's suitor, George Maples, besotted with Linda from way back in high school. Linda could not ignore him because he was sharing the trip with her parents. She took them sightseeing around the town, and to the better restaurants and tourist attractions. They visited the town landmarks: the maritime museum, the botanical gardens, the Civil War battlefields, the many statues of Civil War heroes on horseback, two small Anglican churches from the days of the American Revolution, etc. They all enjoyed the activities that Linda had organized for them and thanked Linda profusely for the excellent way she had taken care of them. When they were all sitting inside their car, George took one of Linda's hands and whispered sweetly in Linda's ear that he'd be back for sure.

The following weeks, George sent her flowers, photographs of him with his parents and with Linda, a box of chocolates, and expensive greeting cards with tender messages of love. One day, he sent her a love poem he had written. It could not compare with the beautiful romantic poems the Captain would send her.

One Sunday, the principal Florida newspaper ran a story about a town in South Florida with a lot to offer tourists and encouraged its readers to travel there to enjoy good food and great beaches, and perhaps take a boat ride out from one of the marinas to enjoy a day fishing or sightseeing. On the front page was a photograph of a dead twenty-foot-long tiger shark lying on the sand flats.

The story informed their readers that a huge tiger shark's dead body appeared one day on the beach, and that four bullets recovered from the body were of the kind commonly used in high power rifles. The writer speculated that the boat owner and the shark had fought a mortal battle on the high seas, and the shark had lost.

That newspaper article was instrumental in getting people talking about visiting those same South Florida coastal towns and enjoying their stay there by partaking in fun activities like swimming, fishing, surfing, and dining out. Visitors thought that this was a great opportunity for all their family members to spend quality time together, deepening and strengthening their ties, while enjoying an extra special good time.

Chapter 15
FINALLY, THERE IS HOPE

There was ferment and optimism flooding hearts in the Cuban-American community in South Florida. There were also expectations of a happy outcome from loyal friends and clients of the Captain residing in coastal Florida and also along the Gulf Coast all the way to New Orleans. They had read the story that the Captain's boat, the Esperanza, was found wedged between huge boulders in a fjord in Iceland, and that the hull showed many embedded teeth from a tiger shark attack, but that the Captain's dinghy was not found! And then there was the photo of the huge tiger shark killed by means of four bullets shot from a high power sniper rifle. The Captain's friends thought it was possible, and credible, that the Captain had shot and killed the tiger shark. They believed that he was alive but lost somewhere.

Immediately there was hope! Friends phoned Linda and Andy with the good news that the Captain was possibly alive and well, and that it was reasonable to think that he had made his home in a town by the seashore in South Florida. Regardless of her doubts of pursuing this new lead, Linda decided to contact the local newspapers in the vicinities of the towns where the shark's dead body had been found and photographed. Linda would ask them to please print a photo she provided. The photo showed Andy, Linda, and the Captain, sitting together around a table in a bar the Captain loved. Andy and Linda thought the photo might spark a flashback within the Captain's mind.

She also requested of the newspaper editors to please print a photo of the Captain (which she was including) with the message that said, *"We, Mario Fernandez's friends, are seeking the whereabouts of our dear friend who has been missing for more than a month and a half. We want to bring him back to his home. Maybe he is using another name. If you recognize him by the photograph, please phone this number or email us at…"*

The local newspapers in South Florida's seaside towns and villages agreed to help them, and they printed the photos and included Linda's "message." Most everyone in the towns along the seashore knew "Mario Fernandez" as "Mario Rodriguez," and Linda started to receive many phone calls and emails telling her that they did recognize the person and that he was a much sought-after boat mechanic named Mario Rodriguez, who worked at a few marinas there. Linda and Andy were exhilarated by the news!

They met to talk about their next steps. Linda knew she stood now at a crossroads. She could follow this lead and join Andy in undertaking the search that could possibly locate the Captain, or she could return home to Birmingham and start a new life there, and the chance to pursue a stable relationship with George Maples that would certainly lead to marriage.

Finally, There is Hope

The Captain had promised marriage and his mother's wedding ring, but these had not materialized. Linda could not accept living day to day in the near future knowing that the Captain kept on navigating the dangerous ocean, courting death and disaster, and perhaps, with time, turning Linda into a young widow. She was not sure if the man she loved was still the same man they'd find at the marina. How much had he changed, and would she still love him in spite of all the changes he may have experienced in his body and mind? She pondered: Why had he not contacted her if he was safe and alive? Had he found another love? Linda questioned whether her relationship with the Captain was worth saving. The only way that she could find out if the Captain was a changed man, and not the man she loved, was to face him and look into his eyes and see what response her presence would elicit.

The towns that replied to their request were located in South Florida between Jupiter and Boca Raton. There were many marinas in the area, and the Captain could certainly be employed and making a living there. They put together a plan. First, they would drive to the towns and villages that replied to their request, moving along the shoreline road, contacting nearby marinas, with the hope that one of them might be employing the Captain. Linda and Andy planned to arrive at the marinas with photos of the Captain at his house, with his friends, on his boat with Andy, on his dinghy, with Linda by his home, and with other friends, hoping all along that a true connection would take place in the mind of Mario Rodriguez when he started reviewing the photos. It was a risky move, and a very delicate approach was needed. Both friends prayed the Captain would not be angry and confused by their request, and then close his eyes and ears to their entreaties. It was now or never.

Chapter 16
RETURN

Psychologists and psychiatrists were very much in contact with the South Florida media as early as 1959. Cubans who had escaped in rafts across the Straits of Florida in the 1960s and later, suffered countless fatalities, and the Miami newspapers, especially, were asked many questions by their readers about the state of mind of rafter friends and relatives. The rafters had floated for days on flimsy rafts at the mercy of stormy winds, huge waves, and relentless shark attacks in order to land in Florida. Tens of thousands of people are thought to have perished in the Florida Straits, and a large but unknown number at the jaws of sharks. Survivors mention shark attacks during their terrible voyages. Some of the rafters saw family members taken by sharks.

Mental health professionals continued their collaboration with the Florida media beyond the 1960s. The media used them to respond to questions from readers concerning the psychic impact on survivors of recent boat accidents in Florida waters. Some of these professionals were contacted by a few of the Captain's friends in a very confidential manner. In their arrangement, it was stipulated that the media should never find out about this matter of the Captain's disappearance and his possible reappearance in coastal South Florida.

The Captain's long time absence from his friends and his lack of communication with people who loved him were brought up as topics for discussion. Questions were asked about the Captain's probable state of mind after having endured the trials and tribulations inherent in trying to survive for more than a month in the grip of a violent ocean. Psychologists and psychiatrists consulted by the Captain's friends informed them that the Captain's lack of recall of his past life was probably due to a partial memory loss. That was all well and good, but for Linda and Andy, it was not enough. They needed additional certainty. "Probably" was not the word they wanted to hear, and they also needed a greater degree of confidence in any proposed diagnosis, and a workable approach to healing the Captain.

Linda and Andy then assembled a team made up of three psychiatrists of renown. These professionals discussed the matter at hand and reached the consensus Linda and Andy were seeking. They agreed that the Captain's lack of communication with his friends and loved ones could only be explained by a partial memory loss suffered by the Captain due to traumatic events he had experienced during his return trip from Tampa. It was their medical opinion that the partial amnesia could be reversed with time, but how quickly differed from person to person.

More than a month had passed since the Captain's disappearance. The three psychiatrists consulted by Linda and Andy believed that enough time had already elapsed for a partial memory recovery to be possible.

For that to happen, a new stressful situation of an emotional nature would need to be presented to the Captain, and they believed that it would provide the needed stimulus for the Captain's mind to recover. Just a minor amount of emotional stress would do, in the same way that in chemical reactions, only tiny amounts of catalysts are required to attain the desired end.

The first part of the plan was put into action. Linda and Andy proposed that they would drive to the places that replied to their request for help. They would move along the shoreline road contacting nearby marinas where the captain was most likely to be employed. When the particular marina was identified, the second part of their plan would be activated, and an "intervention" to return to the Captain all that he had lost in the traumatic voyage home from Tampa would take place. Who could be better suited than his best friends (Linda and Andy) to conduct that intervention?

The three psychiatrists had assured them that the planned intervention to be conducted by Linda and by Andy would provide just the right amount of emotional stress that would return to the Captain the full use of his memory. The suggested approach was that the Captain would be given a number of photographs that showed his past life, everyday experiences, and happy moments with Linda and Andy.

As the Captain examined the photographs, it was believed that he'd experience flashes of recognition in going from one to the next photograph. In doing so, the Captain's emotional load would increase gradually until it reached the desired level. At that time, relief of his emotional stress would instantly take place, and it would shake the foundations of his identity. Then, the miracle of partial memory reversal would take place, and the Captain would regain his full memory.

Linda and Andy agreed that they did not want to scare the Captain away with their request, and so they decided that Linda should be first to talk to him. They met with the management of each of the marinas visited, and asked if Mario Rodriguez was working there. One of the marinas said, "Yes," and took them to a workshop full of gears and engines. The man they saw there, hard at work, was their friend Mario Fernandez. Linda took a few steps toward him, gasped, and gazed at him. She searched his face but did not find even a spark of recognition there. Linda was not deterred. Her expression immediately brightened up with hope as she looked into Mario Rodriguez's eyes, those eyes she knew so well and loved. Linda told him they were looking for a good friend of theirs who had disappeared one day in his boat and was not heard from again.

She continued by asking if he would allow them to show him the photos. He replied, "Yes." So, the photos were placed in his hands. Linda told him his friend was named Mario Fernandez, and everyone called him Captain. When the photos were given to him, he looked at each one of them with care, and then, gradually, his expression altered, his facial factions softened, and his deepest feelings gushed out. Tears appeared in his eyes, and he blurted out, "That is me in the photos! I am Mario Fernandez, the Captain! Linda and Andy, you've always been my best friends. I knew you'd come through for me! Thank you for not forgetting, for searching for me, for not giving up hope!" They held each other for the longest time. They had tears in their eyes. The Captain embraced and kissed Linda and gave a bear hug to Andy. The nightmare was finally over!

When Linda and the Captain had some time to themselves, they knew they needed to talk about issues that seemed to have come between them. They sat together, holding hands, and pondered what they wanted to say to each other. The Captain talked first and told Linda that during his voyage he did not stop thinking about her. Even after suffering a partial memory loss upon reaching land, he knew that his soul mate was waiting somewhere for him, and that is why he did not seek to date any woman in town. The Captain continued speaking and told Linda that he loved her as deeply as ever, and promised that they would always stay together. He held her in his arms and kissed her, and she kissed him back.

Linda pointed out that his voyages took him away from her for long periods of time and were not good in forging a deeper bond between them. They were also quite dangerous, as his voyage to Tampa had proven. He replied that as possible alternatives he could offer his customers single-day chartered sport fishing trips closer to Miami, and also fishing excursions on so-called "party boats" and "drift-boats," charging a fixed fee per person.

He had considered all of these alternatives on board the Esperanza. He told Linda that he thought the best alternative was to hire a good captain that had experienced the Gulf Stream thoroughly and knew where to look for the fish species the clients wished to catch. Good captains know that certain fish species prefer specific water temperatures that may occur only at the edge

A VOYAGE FRAUGHT WITH PERIL: THE **CAPTAIN, LINDA** AND THE **TIGER SHARK**

of the Gulf Stream current where it meets the colder surrounding waters.

He thought, however, that "party boats" and "drift boats" did not pay well enough for the time and effort spent in their use. So, in the final analysis, what was doable was to hire captains with experience that would make one-day trips and the more profitable five-day and ten-day fishing trips possible.

The Captain told Linda that his primary emphasis would be to work as an expert mechanic doing boat and marine engine repairs exclusively. But that didn't mean the Esperanza would need to be sold; rather, it would remain a good source of income for them. Linda and the Captain would use the Esperanza on some weekends to visit places of interest nearby, and thus, re-kindle their romance. Also, it would be there for their children to learn how to navigate the Esperanza. He informed Linda that, at long last, he had finally found his mother's ring, in his dinghy! They would get married right away, and both their incomes would be added to pay for future expenses. They were a reunited couple once more!

The spontaneous overflow of tender amorous feelings for each other kindled a fire in their hearts. He wrapped one arm tightly around her waist, lifting Linda slightly up and then brought her down close to his chest. They looked into each other's eyes, and the Captain kissed her sweetly at first, but then urgently, passionately. Later that same day, Linda wrote a letter to her admirer, George Maples, with the message that she was engaged to a wonderful man she loved very much, and that her heart was fully his.

Chapter 17
AFTERMATH

The three of them drove back home. There were hundreds of people, their friends, waiting by the Captain's house. When they got out of the car, shouts of joy were heard all around! Photographers from an important daily newspaper were there, taking photos and interviewing the Captain, Linda, and Andy. The newspapers in South Florida, the rest of the US, and in the Bahamas, printed the story of the Captain and the many vicissitudes he went through on his return trip: surviving a tropical squall, drifting on the Gulf Stream, and surviving the tiger shark attacks; also, his frightening escape and final duel with the tiger shark and his search for a new identity in a seaside town in South Florida. The newspapers released the news that Mario Fernandez, aka "the Captain," was the person who had shot and killed the rogue tiger shark.

The photos of the dead tiger shark appeared in all the newspapers. The government of the Bahamas studied the strange markings on the dorsal fin of the rogue tiger shark and concluded that it was the same rogue shark that had created such mayhem in their islands.

Accordingly, they sent a check for $100,000, reward money, to Mario Fernandez. The money paid off the outstanding balance on the bank loan for the purchase of the Esperanza, and the boat was now fully theirs!

The Captain proposed marriage to Linda that very night. He proudly presented his mother's wedding ring to her and, on one knee, asked if she would marry him. Linda said, "Yes." Linda's parents were there, and they saw their daughter was ecstatic with joy. They were very happy for them. The Captain and Linda would finally join their future lives together as husband and wife.

After the wedding, the Captain and Linda spent a week in the Virgin Islands. They rented a catamaran and sailed around the islands. The water was clear and the color of aquamarine. Soon afterward, Linda was pregnant. They were pleasantly surprised when the doctors told them she was carrying twins, a baby boy and a baby girl! Linda was thrilled and started working to fix up a room for the babies. It was a double blessing, and they felt truly happy and complete. His great reputation as a marine mechanic followed the Captain back home. He had plenty of customers, and he renewed his association with Andy. Their boat repair business did so well that Andy and he opened a satellite office in New Orleans, and their income stream grew appreciably.

Linda's parents, the Smiths, were pleased with the couple's success and the higher income that their daughter and son-in-law had generated and enjoyed. Linda's father saw matters differently now than before her marriage and urged the Captain to open another subsidiary, but this time in Mobile, Alabama. He offered to become partners in the new venture. The Captain agreed, and soon the Smiths started acting like real in-laws and offered to host the Fernandez children in their home all summer long so the children could get to know their Smith grandparents better, and the Captain and Linda could get to share some private time together.

The Captain saw that people were coming from far away to see him. Now, all of a sudden, people sought his opinion on various matters. There was even talk of making him a candidate for election to a political position in the Miami city government, and possibly running for office representing his district in the Florida State government. It was smooth sailing from then on. They were a happily married couple, with lovely children who adored them. Their future looked auspicious, and they thanked God for that.

Appendix
THE TIGER SHARKS

After his encounter with the tiger shark in Cuba, and impressed by its aggressiveness, Mario realized he needed to know more about them and reached for the shark lectures written by his uncle Carlos Fernandez, a marine biologist and expert on sharks. He also read the scientific articles his uncle had published in science books and magazines.

Mario learned that scientists claimed the giant extinct shark *Carchadoron megalodon* was the ancestor of the great white shark. It had been reported that in 1945, six fishermen embarked from the port of Cojimar, Cuba to find and kill the underwater monster that was devouring their fish and threatening small boats. The crew took off in a small rowboat, armed only with ropes and harpoons. After they hooked the creature, they spent the night and the following day battling it in an epic struggle. When the fishermen finally arrived at the port, the townspeople flocked to observe the catch, a great white shark. It was twenty-one feet long and weighed seven thousand pounds, and all remembered it as "The Monster of Cojimar." Someone even took a photo.

Megalodon could grow to sixty feet (eighteen meters) in length and had a bite more powerful than that of *Tyrannosarus rex*. It had 278 teeth about seven and a half inches long. This sea monster terrorized the ocean from about sixteen million to two million years ago. Mario first learned of this extinct shark from his uncle. Carlos Fernandez, Mario's uncle, was invited by the Smithsonian Institute to give a lecture on extinct sharks. Carlos took Mario with him and paid his travel expenses. When his talk was over, he rented a car and drove to Calvert Cliffs in the state of Maryland. The crumbling cliffs are a famous source of Miocene period fossil marine life.

They descended to the sandy beach hugging the crumbling cliffs and searched around at the cliff's base. Mario was extremely lucky to have found on his first try an impressively large fossil shark tooth. The fossil shark tooth was eight inches long and belonged to the giant of sharks, *Carcharodon megalodon*. Without doubt, that fossil find was an event that fed Mario's interest in sharks. Uncle Carlos had been building up Mario's knowledge of sharks in hopes that someday he would decide to become a marine biologist like himself.

Carlos had no children of his own and considered Mario a son. He hoped that finding the special fossil shark tooth would predispose Mario toward a serious pursuit of academia. He had connections that would facilitate providing a scholarship to Mario for the study of marine science. Even though Mario ultimately did not follow his uncle Carlos's pursuit of science, he always treasured the memory of his uncle and that fossil shark tooth, and when he departed Cuba, it was hidden in his luggage.

Yet, no one knows what ancient shark species was the ancestor of the tiger shark. The differences between the two species of sharks include the shape of their teeth. There were differences in the shapes of the teeth between the great white sharks and the tiger sharks. Great white sharks have sharp triangular serrated teeth (like Megalodon's) but each tiger shark tooth is almost like having several teeth in one space. The sharp primary cusp extends down, ready to tear into prey, and along the primary cusp, or point, are tiny little serrated edges that can saw into the food. The tiger shark has identical upper and lower jaws, and with all these serrated teeth, there's really nothing that the tiger shark can't eat or cut through, including turtle shells.

Mario read that tiger sharks are among the largest species of shark and a top predator of the tropical waters. They get their name from the stripe-like patterns on the sharks' skin. These sharks are widespread throughout tropical and subtropical oceans of the world, in both deep and shallow waters, and appear wherever they want to be, and whenever their hunger demands predation.

Excellent eyesight and acute sense of smell enable the shark to react to faint traces of blood and follow them to their source. Natives of the Caribbean islands consider the tiger shark to be the most dangerous of sharks for two reasons: it is known to swim in schools and therefore to indulge more often in a mob feeding pattern when it finds food in the water, and it unhesitatingly infiltrates shallow waters close to shore where swimmers are likely to be found.

The ability to pick up on low frequency pressure waves enabled the tiger shark to advance toward an animal with confidence, even in murky water. The tiger shark circles its prey and learns its reactions by prodding it with its snout. When attacking, the shark often eats its prey whole. Despite their sluggish appearance, tiger sharks are one of the strongest swimmers of the sharks. Once the shark gets very close, a burst of speed allows it to reach the intended prey before it can escape. It is a fearsome man-eater. Shallow water is not a safety factor. Fatal shark attacks have often occurred in water less than three feet deep.

Adult tiger sharks may grow to thirty feet in length, though they average about sixteen to twenty feet. Scientists estimate that tiger sharks live to be about twelve to twenty years, but that estimate is thought to be on the low side. Young tiger sharks are able to feed on a variety of aquatic animals such as sea turtles, fish, squids, birds, seals, and other sharks. As the tiger sharks grow in size, so does the size of their prey.

Tracking the tiger sharks with satellite tags revealed details about the sharks' secret lives. Some tiger sharks travel close to five thousand miles each year in a round trip to winter in the Caribbean coral reefs, and spend the summer in the mid-North Atlantic open waters, with some sharks reaching as far north as Cape Cod. Previously, it had been thought tiger sharks remained around coastal tropical areas, but the new evidence does not show that.

Springtime is shark time in coastal Florida waters. Along the beach from Boca Raton to Jupiter, Florida, thousands of sharks patrol the waters. Most of these are black tip sharks, which are commonly preyed upon by tiger sharks. Due to the migration of the tiger sharks along the East Coast of the United States, attacks by tiger sharks on humans have taken place. On September 4, 2001, one tiger shark attack off North Carolina's coast stands out as particularly brutal. The man was twenty-eight years old, and his partner was a young lady, twenty-three years old. They lived together in northern Virginia.

The shark attacked them simultaneously, alternating bites. A medical examiner determined that the young man died of massive blood loss caused by multiple shark bites. His lady friend also suffered major injuries, the loss of her left foot and major bites in the left hip and groin areas, but survived the attack. The couple had been swimming close to shore in the afternoon at 6:00 p.m. near Avon, N.C., when the shark struck.

Every single year, great numbers of tiger sharks gather in lagoons in the middle of atolls, and in the shallow waters surrounding islands where the albatrosses nest, and there, make ready to take part in predation of albatross fledglings when baby albatrosses test their wings in flight for the first time. Tiger sharks somehow also know when adult green sea turtles appear in multitudes by the sandy coast of small islands near Australia in order to lay their eggs. Both species are heavily preyed upon annually by mobs of tiger sharks appearing at the right time.

These examples of predation on different prey animals seem to show "advance planning" on the part of the tiger sharks, and that ability is truly remarkable. The tiger shark is not just the dumb, and dangerous garbage can of the sea it is reputed to be. Their capabilities are seemingly superior and undeniable. It is also a fish that can plan and anticipate when and where it might participate in an annual large-meal event, and then show up. The sharks in these instances may be exhibiting a behavior a step above what is called "brute instinct."

CPSIA information can be obtained
at www.ICGtesting.com
Printed in the USA
FFHW020902230519
52610804-58093FF